WITCH OUT OF LUCK

A BLAIR WILKES MYSTERY

ELLE ADAMS

The frisbee hovered in the air, and I waved my wand, directing it at Nathan with a levitation spell. He caught it and threw it back, faster than I'd expected. The frisbee sailed past my head, and I raised my wand and gave it another wave. I was a bit too vigorous with my movement because the frisbee flew wildly off course and plunged into the lake.

"Oops. Might have been a bit too enthusiastic there." I walked to the shore and flicked my wand, levitating the frisbee out of the lake onto the grassy bank.

"You're getting good at that spell," Nathan commented.

Heat rose to my cheeks. "I had to master a levitation spell first, to compensate for being the clumsiest witch on the planet."

Another flick of my wand brought the frisbee into my hand and I threw it at Nathan again. He didn't have a wand, not being paranormal, but he didn't need one. As he caught the frisbee in one hand, he received several admiring glances from the academy students further down the lakeshore.

He jerked his head at them. "At this rate, you'll be joining their Sky Hopper game in no time at all."

"Please, no. Helen's already tried to recruit me to supervise the academy's big game at the end of the month. I have to sneak in and out the back door of the witches' HQ to avoid her."

The only activity I hated more than playing team sports was *watching* team sports, especially if there was still a risk of being hit in the face by a projectile. Sky Hopper was a complicated game involving two teams, in which the aim was for each team to pass a series of hoops along a row of players without the opposing team taking the hoops away first. There'd already been at least one argument among the students by the lake about who got to be the Vultures—some of the most important members of the team whose goal was to steal the hoops from the opposing players.

Nathan chuckled. "You never know unless you try."

The frisbee soared above my head. I hopped, missed, and snapped the fingers of my right hand, transforming into fairy mode. My wings came out, beating, and I flew high enough to catch it.

"That's cheating," he said teasingly. "Not all of us can fly."

"I'd rather fly this way than mount a broomstick." I landed on the shore again and tossed the frisbee back. He caught it by his fingertips, and a cheer rose from the students.

Further down the lakeshore, a new group of broomstick-riding witches and wizards approached in a cloud of bright colour. The High Fliers had shown up for their latest practise session. While the academy only held its broomstick contests when there was warm weather, the High Fliers operated in all seasons, including raging storms. Health and safety warnings weren't really their thing. They also wore vividly bright hats and cloaks despite the weather and were currently engaged in some kind of exercise involving people hopping from one broom to the next in mid-air above the lake. The lake might be pretty, but it was also filled with sirens, biting water imps, and who knew what else. The High Fliers took living dangerously to a whole new level.

Shaking my head, I returned my attention to Nathan. Our schedules were both so crowded that this was the first time we'd had the time for a date by the lake all summer. Nathan's job as the town's head of security kept him busy, while I had summer classes almost every day. Even today, I was supposed to be practising for my upcoming exam, but Madame Grey had suggested I might get to skip a grade if I kept going at my current rate. It was a welcome change from my rocky start to witchcraft, even if I was still the only adult witch in the entire town who didn't have an academy diploma. Madame Grey, leader of the Meadowsweet Coven and the witch who owned the entire town of Fairy Falls, had done so much to make me feel welcome since my arrival here a few months ago. I didn't want to let her down by failing my next exam.

There was a splash and a yelp from further along the shore. It looked like one of the academy students had tried to imitate the High Fliers' broom-hopping stunt and knocked both himself and the person on the other broom into the lake instead. It was bolstering to see that accidents still happened to the most accomplished wizards and witches in Fairy Falls, not just newbies like me.

A cluster of broomsticks descended behind Nathan and me as we continued to throw the frisbee to one another. The academy students had given in to the inevitable invasion of their airspace by the High Fliers and had instead decided to watch the show. Loud music blasted from further up the bank, where someone had brought out the magical equivalent to a set of speakers. Someone else passed around cups of wine. Soon, the riotous sounds of a party surrounded our once-quiet spot. Heads bobbed above the water as half the merpeople in the lake arrived to enjoy the fun, and one of them ducked when my frisbee nearly hit him on the head. Oops.

I flicked my wand and levitated the frisbee over to Nathan, who caught it in his hand. "I think that's enough for one day."

"Agreed." I walked over to him at the lake's shore, and he handed me the frisbee. "Today was nice. We should do this more often."

Dating someone with as busy a schedule as the town's leading security guard had its downsides as well as its perks, but I had to admit, life was good. I was improving my skill in magic with each passing day, my workload was manageable, and—oh, I was dating the hottest, most considerate guy in town. How had I got this lucky?

There was just one *slight* thing bothering me: I hadn't heard from my father in weeks.

That my father might be a fairy held captive in the most notorious paranormal prison in the north of England hadn't exactly been my first assumption when I'd wondered about my birth family growing up. My dad had omitted to tell me *why* he was in jail, or why it'd taken him twenty-five years to get in touch with me. But despite the distance separating us, we'd begun to connect. Sort of. And then he'd dropped a bombshell on me in the form of the following message: *If Inquisitor Hare has targeted you, Blair, leave Fairy Falls. Your life depends on it.*

Nearly a month had passed since Inquisitor Hare, leader of the paranormal hunters and owner of the prison where my dad had been locked away for the last few years, had been in town. There had been no sightings of a single hunter since then. But when I'd written back to my dad to ask why I had to flee, he'd repeated the same message. And then he'd stopped replying at all.

Since the only way to contact my father was by sending notes via pixie, it wasn't like I could stride into the prison and ask him. The only reason I knew he was there at all was due to the elf king, who'd admitted to sheltering my dad in the woods a few years ago. My father had claimed to be on the run from someone dangerous but had got caught and arrested shortly after without ever mentioning who was chasing him. He claimed he couldn't tell me anything important in a letter, but that left me at a loose end. I'd *almost* got to meet him in person on the summer solstice, the single day when the hunters allowed fairies to leave the prison under supervision, but then a man-eating monster had got loose in the woods. Perhaps my dad had a point about the town not being entirely safe, considering the level of trouble I ran into on a daily basis. But I wouldn't trade this new life for the world.

Nathan and I walked up the lakeshore and found a new quiet spot to watch the sun sink lower over the lake, turning the water's surface into gold. I could never get tired of the view. Or the man next to me, come to that. His hand intertwined with mine, and I turned from the lake to find him smiling at me. "Blair? You were a mile away."

"I guess you'd rather I was paying attention to you than the view?"

He laughed. "The view *is* nice, so I won't be too offended." Then he leaned over and kissed me.

Cheering came from the students and my face flamed. "Maybe we should have gone somewhere more private."

"I don't mind," he said. "I actually had something I wanted to talk to you about, Blair."

"Oh?" It couldn't be serious, or he'd have told me right away.

"Yes," he said. "My family's coming to town. They're very keen to meet you."

"Ah." My heart jumped in my chest. "Uh… are you sure?"

"Positive," he said. "It's not an inspection, don't worry. Just a family visit."

Nathan's family owned one of the local branches of the paranormal hunters, the one closest to town. After his dad had retired, his brother had taken over, and Nathan was the only member of his immediate family who didn't work for them. "Uh, which family exactly?"

"My dad, brothers, and sister," he said. "My sister's excited to get to know you."

"This is the sister who loves bubble wrap, right?" That was about the only thing I might have in common with a family of paranormal hunters—unless they also turned out to be Harry Potter fans. I'd got the impression Nathan was the odd one out in his family since he'd decided he'd rather work as a security guard for Fairy Falls instead of hunting criminals. The hunters policed wayward paranormals, from catching serial killers to putting down rabid werewolves. And arresting fairies who broke the law. Even if they were off-duty, I'd have to be on my best behaviour. Let's just say the hunters and their leader hadn't had pleasant things to say about the state of things in Fairy Falls.

"Yes," he said. "I hope it's not too much to ask for you to try not to do anything that might alarm them."

"You mean, magic." I had fewer accidents than I used to, but I still hadn't quite broken the habit of casting the wrong spell when I was stressed or panicking. "Okay. No accidentally turning people transparent or creating disco balls."

"You haven't done that for a while."

"Nope, but it sometimes happens when I'm nervous. I guess lately I haven't had reason to be."

He smiled. "I'm glad. I was worried for a while that your

time in this town would be fraught with chaos for the long-term."

I shrugged. "It's fine. I'm a fairy witch with weird powers and a weirder cat. I'd be worried if things *did* settle."

Though I wasn't complaining about the calm, the chance to hang out with Nathan by the peaceful lake…

…the peaceful lake, where someone was screaming.

Oh, no.

I turned towards the noise. "What's going on over there?"

"Someone probably fell in the lake." But he let go of my hand and got to his feet.

"That doesn't sound like the scream of someone having fun." I peered through the scattered crowd of students to pinpoint the direction of the noise. "Did someone fall off a broomstick again?"

"They put the brooms away a while ago." Nathan walked up the path, and I moved to join him.

A number of students had gathered at the edge of the route leading to the falls, where the forest bordered the path on the left.

Nathan's long-legged stride reached them first. "What's going on?"

"Terrence is missing," said a blond girl. "Did you see anyone wander into the woods?"

"No," I said. "But we weren't looking that way."

"Are you sure he went into the woods?" Nathan asked.

"That's the last time I saw him," said the girl. My lie-sensing power told me she was telling the truth.

"He couldn't have gone far," Nathan said. "Everyone knows not to go past the falls, don't they?"

Not drunken teenagers, though. Or… well, me. I'd visited the elven king deep in the forest a few times. Not that I'd be admitting it now.

"I saw him go up there," said a pale brunette girl who

wore an upside-down witch's hat, pointing uphill. "He and Casey were arguing."

"That was ages ago," protested a pale young man with a shock of dark brown hair. He'd cut up his long navy-blue cloak that formed the academy's uniform to make it look like a superhero cape.

"We'll look," I said hastily, a little worried that if they tried to follow in their inebriated state, they might trip right over the edge of the path into the lake. There was no fence on the right-hand side and the path became more unsteady the closer you got to the falls. "It's easy to get lost if you wander too far into the woods."

Nathan took the lead uphill. "If not, maybe he's swimming in the lake."

"Or at the falls?" I suggested. "Let's have a look around."

We walked up the path alongside the lake, trees bordering us on our left. The hill steepened until the path forked in two. On the left, it wound away deeper into the woods. On the right, the path turned rocky and steepened, leading down to the falls. I had good memories from here—my first kiss with Nathan came to mind—but bad ones, too. Like the narrow escape I'd had from Mrs Dailey and the small group of hunters who'd been prowling around the woods on her behalf. They'd been reprimanded by their bosses and removed from duty, but I remembered the fear of hiding behind a tree and hoping they wouldn't spot me.

There's nothing here that shouldn't be, Blair. We're safe.

Nathan stopped as we reached the fork in the path. "Maybe we should split up here. Do you want to search the falls?"

"Sure, but I hope he didn't go that way," I answered. "It's hard not to trip on that path even when you're sober." Or when you had two left feet like I did.

"Or you can take the woodland path instead," he said. "But I wouldn't want you to get lost. It'll be dark soon."

"No, I'll check the falls. Don't forget I have wings." I snapped my fingers and my wings came out once again. "See you in five, okay?"

"Sure." He waved me off, making his way down the forest path. An uneasy flutter went through me. I understood why he didn't want me going into the forest alone. Elves, shifters and other paranormals wandered the paths and it was easy to get lost. A drunken teenage wizard would probably get more sympathy for wandering onto shifter territory than the average person, but you never really knew. As for the elves, they were fiercely protective of their territory, and trespassing would get you chased off by a group of terrifying spear-wielding four-foot-tall soldiers. Admittedly, expecting drunken teenagers to follow the rules was pretty much a non-starter. Still, I'd have thought they'd have a little more caution, given that the falls had been under close watch this summer after a monster had been set loose to terrorise the elves a few months ago.

I climbed down the path leading to the falls, halting when I spotted two people coming the opposite way. Both were under five feet tall, wore bark-coloured clothes, and had pointed ears jutting from their dark hair. Weird. The elves never came this close to the lake. I'd thought they preferred to pretend nobody else lived near the woods at all.

"Blair Wilkes," growled one of them, spotting me. He was called Bramble, and the two of us weren't exactly friends. More reluctant acquaintances. I didn't recognise his companion, a taller elf with wispy brown hair.

"Hi," I said to Bramble. "What're you doing so close to the falls?"

He scowled and continued to climb the slope. "Is it of any concern to you?"

"There's a human missing in the woods," I told him. "Seen anyone? He's a teenage wizard, probably drunk."

"It's not our job to police your fellow humans, Blair Wilkes." He beckoned to his partner, and the two of them vanished into the forest.

That's friendly. Shaking my head, I continued to walk down the steepening path. The part of the forest closest to the falls technically belonged to the witches, but anyone was allowed to use certain paths in and out of the woods.

I climbed down some more, using my wings to fly down the steepest parts, and spotted another small figure sitting on a ledge above the lake. He swayed as he sat, singing to himself in a low, melancholy voice. A bottle dangled from his fingertips and his hair and clothes looked unkempt. At first, I thought it was that notorious drunken elf who Alissa sometimes dealt with at the hospital when he'd got into escapades. He did look familiar, but it was difficult to tell from this angle. The only way to the falls was to walk past him and I didn't want to startle him into falling off the ledge, so I cleared my throat to announce my presence.

The elf looked up at me. "Human," he growled. "Go away."

"Sorry, I need to get down here. Were you at the party?" Was it him who Bramble and the others had been talking to?

When he didn't respond, I carried on climbing down the path. In a sudden bound, he was on his feet. He made it two steps before slipping, and I caught his arm before he fell.

"Don't touch me," he growled. "Human filth."

"If you want to fall to your death, be my guest." I let go of his arm and edged past him. *Guess he wasn't at the party, then.*

The path turned to a rocky slope leading down to the surging waterfall. Nobody could walk down here on unsteady feet, not without falling, but I doubted the elf would let me carry him to safer ground. I used my wings to jump down the last few metres until the ground flattened.

On my left-hand side, the magnificent Fairy Falls flowed into a foaming river which joined the lake when it left the cave. Glittering spray drenched me as I walked closer—and a body lay face-down in the water, wearing the cloaked uniform of the academy.

Oh, no.

2

A head popped out of the river before the floating body, and a blue-haired merman looked up at me, his eyes huge and round. "He's not breathing."

"Help me get him out—hang on." I grabbed my wand and levitated the body out of the water. I'd never tried the spell on a human before, but there was no way I could single-handedly carry the dead weight of that waterlogged cloak. It'd be hard to get him up the slope, too, and I had no first aid skills to speak of. Where was Alissa when I needed her?

I flicked my wand and the teenager's body landed on the bank. His eyes were closed, and while the crash of the falls made it hard to tell if he was breathing or not, my paranormal-sensing power was oddly quiet. It almost always worked in the background, telling me the truth of every person I met. Unless… unless that person was dead.

"Hey!" I shouted up the hill. "Hey! Someone help!"

The merman leaned over the bank and flicked his tail anxiously. "I'm sorry, but I think he's dead."

"Did you find him here?" I asked. "Was he alone?"

"I did," he said, his eyes downcast. "He was by the falls. I didn't see anyone else around."

"I'll get him back to the others."

Crossing my fingers that my magical skills didn't fail, I flicked my wand and the student's body floated uphill. Glad of my wings, I flew close behind him, trying to hold my wand hand steady—it would not help the situation if my levitation spell broke. To my relief, the drunken elf seemed to have disappeared into the woods.

Nathan appeared at the top of the slope to meet me. "Blair?"

"I need a hand," I said, my wand hand trembling with the effort of holding it still.

"I've got him." Nathan caught the wizard's body in his arms. "He's not breathing."

"I know." I hurried up the bank to join him. The students had gathered at the foot of the hill, drawn by the noise. "He was in the water by the falls—a merman found him."

We climbed downhill to meet the students and Nathan laid the body down. The students gathered closer, all wearing shocked expressions. Wands flashed, voices shouted, and I squeezed through the crowd to Nathan's side. "I'm guessing he drowned, but I'm no expert. Is there a healer around?"

"I'm a healer," said a female teenage witch with dark skin and braided hair. Tears gleamed in her eyes. "He's dead. I don't understand why he went down to the falls alone."

"Was he alone, though?" I asked, scanning the crowd. "Didn't someone say they saw him arguing with another student?"

"I don't know," said the girl, tears spilling over. "None of us would have let him drown."

"It wasn't an accident," said a tall teenage boy with dreadlocks. "See those sirens over there? Their magic can lure people into the water."

"They're miles off," the girl protested. "He didn't disappear that long ago."

"When was the last time you saw him?" Nathan asked.

"Ten minutes," one of the students said.

"Twenty."

"I haven't seen him for at least an hour."

Their voices clashed—then a bang and a flash of light went off like a firecracker and everyone jumped. A tall blond witch approached the students: Helen, one of the teachers at the academy. The crowd parted to let her through, her long coal-black cloak swirling around her ankles and embossed with the academy's insignia.

"How did this happen?" she asked.

More voices rose, drowning one another out as everyone tried to explain at the same time. Another flash ignited as Helen waved her wand over the body, and the voices faded to murmurs.

Helen tried several spells on the body before retreating, talking into her phone. Probably calling the police, if nobody had already done it.

I turned to Nathan. "I'm not sure there's anything we can do here."

"Blair?" Helen spotted me and made her way over. "They're saying you found his body."

"A merman found him under the falls," I told her. "I think he must have fallen into the river there and drowned."

She nodded, her mouth turning down at the corners. "Those falls are treacherous if you're not careful. The police are on their way."

And that's my cue to leave. I was not the head of the police's favourite person, let's put it that way. Nathan was his equal, technically, but he was head of town security, not law enforcement. Nobody but Steve the grumpy gargoyle wanted *that* job.

Considering Steve's usual approach to a crisis, he'd throw the blame at the wrong person if it turned out Terrence's death wasn't an accident. I'd had a recent stint in a cell and had no desire to repeat the experience.

"Did you see anyone else in the water?" asked Helen.

"There was nobody there." Except for a drunken elf, that is. And Bramble and the others, but they were nowhere near the falls and would have no reason to push a human into the water. Right?

Nope. I definitely don't want to get involved in this.

Nathan cleared his throat. "I'll walk you home," he said. "Before Steve gets here."

"Won't he want to talk to you?"

He shook his head. "I'm not on duty. If he finds out you found the body… you don't want him to know that, right?"

"No, but I saw a few elves on the path by the falls. Right near where I found the body. They don't normally come this close to the lake, do they?"

He frowned. "Not to my knowledge, no."

"We can walk back through the woods," I said. "Maybe one of them saw what happened."

"You need an invitation to go to their territory," he reminded me.

"Yeah, but I don't plan on annoying the king again," I said. "Still, it's worth a look."

The elf king and I were acquaintances, thanks to his brief meeting with my father, but I wouldn't call us friends. If I asked what his people had been doing by the lake, he'd tell me it was none of my business. Who even knew why the elves did anything?

Nathan and I walked back through the woods, but no elves materialised. We spotted several gargoyles flying overhead when we emerged from the trees, their huge wings spread wide. Gargoyles formed the entirety of Fairy Falls's law enforcement and a fair portion of the town's security, too, though the force had recently expanded to include a larger security team led by Nathan himself. I had an inkling they'd end up calling him to patrol by the lake tonight.

"I hope it was an accident," I muttered as we reached the end of my road. "As sad as it is, we don't need any more drama. Are you sure your family aren't bringing more hunters with them?"

"Positive," he said. "They're staying from tomorrow until the weekend. I hope that's okay, Blair."

"Sure," I said. He wanted me to meet his family. If I put the hunter issue aside, that must mean a new step in our relationship, right? It wasn't like I had a family for him to meet. Except for my foster parents, but they were off water-skiing in Australia and had no idea the paranormal world even existed. "I have a magic lesson tomorrow, but I should be free in the evening."

"We'll work something out." He kissed me goodbye, and we parted ways.

This really is a new step. The idea of meeting Nathan's family was possibly scarier than the idea of meeting more of the hunters. The hunters I'd met, with the exception of their terrifying leader Inquisitor Hare, had been bumbling idiots. Nathan had used the same descriptor for his siblings once before, and while I'd mentally prepared for them not to like me, I hadn't expected to meet them in person so soon.

I entered the huge manor house which had become my new home and walked down the hallway, unlocking the door on the right that led to the ground-floor flat I shared with Alissa, Madame Grey's granddaughter.

"Hey, Blair," said Alissa, as I walked in. She lay on the sofa, stroking Roald, her familiar. "You look kinda frazzled."

"Two reasons," I said. "Firstly, one of the students from the academy drowned in the lake."

Her face fell. "Really? Oh, no."

I sat down in the armchair. "Yeah, he fell into the river by the falls. I had to leave before the police showed up, since I'm the one who found the body."

"Oh, Blair." She sighed. "As long as it was just an accident this time..."

"I hope so, because I'm meeting Nathan's family in a day or two," I said. "I don't think they want to meet me from the other side of a prison cell door."

Her eyes popped out. "His family—the hunters?"

"It's just a family visit, that's all." *I hope.* "He said they're coming tomorrow and staying all week."

"Wow," she said. "Have you even been to Nathan's place yet?"

"No," I said. "He's been working all summer." And with his family around all week, I suspected we wouldn't get another date for a while.

Sky walked over to me and rubbed against my legs. I stroked him behind the ears. Sky wasn't my familiar, more my adopted fairy cat partner. He was a little black cat with one white paw, one blue eye and one grey.

"Want to meet Nathan's family?" I asked him. "He has three cats. Maybe you'll get along."

I didn't know how much Sky could actually understand of what I said, but he purred. I was also less than certain that anyone with ties to the hunters had 'meet a weird fairy cat' on their bucket list, but you never knew.

———

After work the next day, I went straight to my magic lesson once I'd dropped off my work gear at home. Since there were a lot of summer school classes on, I had lessons whenever Rita could fit me in and often ended up supervising Rebecca, the town's newest witch-in-training. Rebecca Dailey had developed her magical skills later than most, partly due to her scheming, manipulative mother, but her powerful ability to alter people's personalities meant she'd been put in accelerated training. Like me. Except I was twenty-five, not eleven.

I had to admit I'd actually enjoyed helping Rebecca with magic. It was refreshing to meet someone with less experience than I had, if nothing else. But she wasn't in the classroom when I got there. Instead, Rita waited for me, her curly red hair standing on end and a harassed expression on her face.

"I just had to supervise sixty tween witches and wizards learning to mount broomsticks for the first time," she said in explanation. "Helen usually does that, but she's been at the police office for most of the day."

"Yikes." I was glad that wasn't on the curriculum for me. "Oh—she was giving a statement on Terrence's death, right?"

"Yes. Why, you weren't there, were you?"

"Nathan and I were by the lake yesterday," I explained. "The student drowned."

"So it seems," she said. "Helen was dealing with Steve, which left *me* to deal with her pupils. When I agreed to it, I didn't know she'd offered to teach the entire upcoming class of academy students basic broomstick lessons."

"Oh, dear." I couldn't picture Rita on a broomstick. The red-haired witch with all her bangles and accessories had always struck me as the sort of person who wanted both feet planted firmly on the ground.

"Now, for your progress," she said. "Madame Grey thinks you're ready to take the Grade Three theory exam at the end of the month. You're skipping a grade, but we've covered enough material that there shouldn't be any surprises. It's best to fit in your exams before the academy students go back to school. Is that okay?"

"Sounds good," I said. "And the practical exam? There's one of those, right?"

"There is," she said. "Grade Two requires a basic potions exam and another to test your use of spells. However, if you want to advance to Grade Three, you'll also need to pass at least one 'other' skill. I suggested to Helen that you might like to take one of her beginner's broomstick lessons."

Ack. Looks like I spoke too soon. "But I have wings," I said. "And Seven Millimetre Boots. Isn't that enough?"

"Blair, you never know when you're going to need a particular skill," she said sternly. "If you want to advance to Grade Three, you'll need to know how to mount and dismount a broom at a minimum. It's that or sign up to a different extracurricular class with the other students at your level."

I grimaced. If I struggled to keep up with a curriculum designed for six-year-olds, I'd be seriously questioning whether I belonged among witches. Even if I was only half of one.

"I'll speak to Helen. I didn't know she was in charge of that department." I knew she worked at the academy, but she volunteered with all kinds of extracurriculars, too. "You know I can barely stay upright with two feet on the ground, though."

"Blair, I'm not asking you to join the High Fliers. You'll do fine."

I hope. So much for dodging Helen's rigorous attempts to sign me up to help out at the academy's Sky Hopper contest. My only experience with brooms so far had involved me trying to wrestle Alissa off the end of one after a personality-altering spell had caused her to re-join the High Fliers. I'd nearly drowned both of us in the lake in the process. Not my finest hour. Putting me in charge of supervising small children on brooms was like asking my cat to behave at a dinner party.

"Good," said Rita. "You're to meet Helen after your lesson. Now, turn to Chapter Four."

———

Once my theory lesson was over, I left the classroom and went looking for Helen. It wasn't hard to find her, sitting in an empty room surrounded by books. When she wasn't running extracurriculars, she was engaging in night classes of her own. Helen made the word 'overachiever' look like an understatement.

The blond witch looked up from her stack of textbooks. "Blair! It's so good to see you."

"Ah, Rita sent me to find you," I said, before she tried to rope me into playing classroom assistant to a bunch of wand-wielding teenagers. "She said you'd be able to fit me into a beginner's broomstick lesson."

"Oh!" Her whole face lit up. "You want to learn? I can definitely do that for you. There aren't any beginner's classes starting this week, but if it's just the basics, I can teach you myself."

"Oh, really?" I asked. "I don't want to give you too much trouble."

"It's no trouble," she said. "I enjoy helping new fliers. Judging and supervising games is fun, but there's something special about seeing someone take to the skies for the first time. You'll be able to fly… that opens a lot of doors for you."

"Not many doors in the sky," I said. "Uh, anyway, I guess it won't hurt to know how to mount a broom if I ever need to." I couldn't imagine I would, but if it took humiliating myself on a broom to become a full-fledged witch, I'd do it.

"Yes, you'll be able to play referee at our games!" she said. "We're always looking for volunteers."

"Uh… best see if I can actually mount a broomstick first," I said quickly. "If I can't get off the ground, I won't be much use as a referee."

She laughed. "I'm sure you'll be a natural. Want to start now? I have a free hour before dinner. Unless you have a date with Nathan?"

"Ah, no, I don't," I said. "He's busy. I guess we should get it over with… er, I mean, no time like the present, right?"

Despite my reservations, there wouldn't be anyone else in classes at this time. No witnesses to see me make a fool of myself. Perfect.

"Good. The broomsticks are in the storeroom. I have a spare key. Can't have students stealing those brooms and zipping around town, can we?"

Since Alissa had stolen one while under the influence of Rebecca's personality-altering spell, locking the brooms up was probably the best idea. Granted, it hadn't stopped the academy students' drunken stunts at the lake yesterday.

Helen left the classroom and we made our way to the storeroom. I envied her energy. After a long day at work and an advanced theory class, I was more in the mood for a nap than a broomstick lesson. On the other hand, I'd come to enjoy flitting around using my fairy wings. A broom couldn't be that different, right?

"The back garden will be perfect," she said, passing me a broom. "There's plenty of space."

We carried the broomsticks out through the back doors of the witches' headquarters. A spacious lawn filled the garden, which should hopefully make for a soft landing if I fell off. I checked my wand was within easy reach before taking my position beside the broomstick.

"It's easy." Helen swung a leg over her broom and was in the air a moment later. "See?"

I blinked at her. "Could you demonstrate again, more slowly?"

"Sure." She bounded off the broomstick onto the lawn. "It's simple. Just stand like this, grip the broom between your legs—" She did so—"and when you're ready to fly, tap the end with your wand."

"You didn't use your wand just then," I pointed out.

"That's the advanced class." She grinned at me. "You'll get to that later."

I pulled out my wand and sat on the broom, awkwardly gripping it between my legs. Then I tapped the end. The broom didn't move. Maybe it knew I didn't want to be in the air.

Another tap, more aggressive. "Broom…. fly."

The broom tipped backwards, knocking me onto my back. "Ow."

"You okay there, Blair?"

I lifted my head. "Sure. I take it getting my wings out would be cheating?"

"In the exam? Yes. But if it helps you now, I won't tell anyone." She winked.

Ugh. I guess I'd better learn to do this by the book, then.

I got to my feet, mounted the broom, and tapped the end. The broom rose at an angle, and once again, I slid backwards and toppled onto the grass. Muffled laughter came from behind me. So much for no witnesses.

I risked a glance over my shoulder to see who was amused at my misfortune and spotted a dozen children hiding in the bushes.

Helen flapped a hand at them. "Go on, run along and meet your parents."

More laughter from the other bushes. Adult laughter. Their parents were watching and laughing at me, too. My face heated up. I wished we'd gone over to the lake instead. Then I could have hidden in the woods until everyone went away.

Gritting my teeth, I picked up the broom. "Don't like fairies, do you?" I muttered to it. "Tough. I'm witch enough to fly, and you're going to do as I say."

"Why is she talking to the broom?" asked one of the little girls, loudly.

I mounted the broom. When it jerked into the air, I abruptly fell off again to another cloud of laughter. "Ow. Can the broom sense that I'm nervous?"

"No," Helen said. "It's a spelled object, not sentient."

"It sure doesn't seem to want me in the sky." I climbed to my feet again. "Is it because I'm left-handed? Or is my fairy magic interfering?"

"I doubt it. You just need to keep trying."

I practised. The broom refused to cooperate with me. Finally, in a fit of frustration, I de-glamoured before hitting the end of the broom hard enough for sparks to burst from the end of my wand. There was a rising gasp from the small children, then the broom shot into the air.

Without me.

If not for my wings, I'd have fallen out of the air. As it was, I hovered on the spot as the broom plummeted back to earth and hit Helen on the head.

I dropped, beating my wings, and landed beside her. "Helen, are you okay?"

She looked up dizzily. "Hmm?"

"Oh, no. I can call Alissa." I snapped my fingers and turned back into human mode again, grabbing my phone.

"No need." Rita crossed the lawn, waved her wand, and Helen's dazed expression disappeared. "You might have a sore head for a bit."

"I'm sorry!" My face flamed. "This is why I shouldn't be flying."

Helen shook her head. "No, you just need to be more prepared next time. Try again."

With Rita watching expectantly, I was outnumbered, so I grabbed the broom and swung my leg over the side. Drawing in a breath, I tapped the end.

This time, I managed to hang onto the broom as it rose into the air a few inches. "Yes!" I didn't quite have the courage to dance in mid-air, but I did a silent celebratory dance in my head.

Steering it back to earth was another story. I leaned forwards, and the broom pitched me off sideways. I tumbled to the ground in time for the broom to hit *me* in the head. I looked up dazedly to screaming laughter from the small children.

"Go home," Rita said to them. "Blair, are you okay?"

"Great." I rubbed my forehead. "I don't think I'll be joining the High Fliers anytime soon."

"Maybe you should try another day," Helen said. "You're not bad for a beginner, at all. I've seen worse."

From small children. It was hard to concentrate when I was being gawked at by onlookers waiting for me to fall off my broom anyway. I picked up the broom and accompanied Helen back into the witches' headquarters.

A tall witch wearing a red hat accosted her on the way to the store cupboard. "Oh, Helen, I was looking for you. Can I have a word?"

"Sure." Helen turned to me. "Blair, can you take both brooms back?"

"Okay." I took the broomstick from her, and returned

them both to the store cupboard, giving them a thorough glare before closing the door.

Helen showed up a moment later, her sunny demeanour gone. If anything, she looked almost as upset as she had at the lake.

"Are you okay?" She might have put me through broomstick hell, but I'd asked her to do it, after all.

She flicked her wand and the store cupboard locked itself. "Yes… it's Terrence. The verdict is that he didn't die by accident."

My heart sank. "Really?"

"His talent was water manipulation," she explained, putting her wand away. "In some cases, magical talents can activate even if the wizard is unconscious, so it's unlikely that he drowned by accident. Madame Grey confirmed it."

"Oh, no." I hadn't known it was possible for someone to have a skill that worked even when they'd passed out.

She exhaled in a sigh. "The problem is, we don't have any real idea of who might have done it, and I don't want Steve terrorising everyone at the academy if he gets wind that it wasn't an accident."

"What—he thinks a student did it?"

"Maybe," she said. "I actually wondered if you could do me a favour, Blair. You know when people are lying, right?"

"Oh," I said, caught off guard. "Uh, yeah. I'm not a detective. And people have got around my lie-sensing power before."

She bit her lip. "It's just… well. We're having trouble piecing together what happened by the lake. I wondered if you could come and talk to the students after tomorrow's lesson. or before. Wait, you work at Dritch & Co, don't you?"

"Yes, but I might have plans tomorrow evening." Like meeting Nathan's parents, for instance. "I can come in the morning, though, but it'd have to be before nine."

"Classes start at eight. That's perfect."

The poor kids, being dragged out of bed at that hour in the summer holidays. Still, I felt bad for Helen. She clearly cared about her job, and now she was having to deal with the death of one of her students.

I'd probably regret this, but at this rate, I'd need weeks of lessons before I mastered the broomstick. I owed her at least one favour for helping me out.

"All right," I said. "I'll talk to them."

3

Early the next morning, I set off for the academy. The town's premier witchcraft institution was a brick building with its exterior decorated with a symbol of two wands crisscrossing. In August, there weren't as many students crowding behind the wrought-iron fences as there would be during term time, though on the other side of the fence, a small group of teenagers stood in a huddle, talking among themselves.

Helen spotted me and smiled. As I walked to the gates, she unlocked them with a wave of her wand, inviting me into the school grounds.

"The students have to come here every day for registration, so everyone who was at the lake the other night is in the grounds," she said to me in an undertone. "They know you're here to talk to them, so there won't be any misunderstandings."

Good. I was already regretting dragging myself out of bed to play detective when I'd told Nathan I wouldn't do anything to stir up trouble this week. Even if I owed Helen a favour, things had a tendency to spiral out of control wherever I was involved. I'd made it through a whole month without an argument with Steve the Gargoyle and I'd prefer not to break my streak.

Helen approached the huddle of robe-wearing students. "Hey, everyone," she said brightly. "This is Blair. She's a detective."

Ah, no.

"She isn't," said a teenage boy. "She works at that weird place where the lady was accused of murdering someone."

Ack. "I do work for Dritch & Co," I admitted. "That means I find suitable candidates for paranormal clients. Anyway, Helen asked me to come here and talk to you about what happened at the lake on Sunday. I think you'd rather talk to me than Steve, right?"

A few murmurs of agreement passed through the group.

"What d'you want to know?" asked the teenage boy.

"Who was the last person to see Terrence, before he died?" I asked.

Several people spoke up, pointing fingers. Even my lie-sensing power wouldn't work on a dozen people talking at once.

"Okay, one at a time." I turned to the nearest student. He had a mop of dark brown hair and while he must have fixed his cloak so it no longer resembled a superhero cape, I recognised him as the boy who'd been accused of arguing with Terrence before his death. "Did you know Terrence?"

"We were friends, yeah." He looked as irritated and tired as Helen. "The police have already spoken to me. I didn't push him into the water."

Truth.

"You were arguing, though," said a girl with blond hair. "Weren't you?"

His mouth turned down at the corners. "We were drunk. It was a stupid argument."

"About what?" I asked.

"The sirens," supplied the blond girl. "You were arguing because he wanted to swim off and flirt with the sirens."

"Right," he said. "Yeah. He's—he was an idiot. Everyone knows not to flirt with the sirens. There was one who kept coming close to shore and he kept saying he was going to swim off with her."

True.

"But he didn't, right?" I asked.

"I didn't see," the boy said. "I wouldn't have thought he would, but you know, he was drunk."

True... as far as I could tell.

"Did you see him go in the water?" I asked. "With the siren?"

"Like I said, I lost track of him when he stormed off after we argued," the boy said.

True. "Did he go down to the falls?" I asked, thinking of the elves. "You must have known that he was in no fit state to climb down that path. It's tough enough when you're sober."

"For some people, maybe," he said. "No, I'm not his babysitter. Stop looking at me like that, Clarence. I didn't kill him."

Truth. I saw Helen looking at me and shook my head, just slightly.

"But he had the ability to manipulate water, right?" I asked the group. "That means he can't have drowned by accident, doesn't it?"

"Not necessarily," said the blond girl. "If he was drunk enough, he might have forgotten to use magic."

"I'm surprised he even got to the falls without breaking his neck," added one of the others.

The boy scowled. "Yeah, okay, okay. Maybe his power stopped working. Or the sirens sang..."

"The siren song might have made him forget his magic?"

Maybe I'd need to speak to the sirens, not the students. I'd dealt with a siren before who'd accidentally killed her human lover. A drunk wizard, even one who had an affinity with water, would be an easy target.

"You can't forget your magic," put in someone else. "Survival instinct kicks in."

"I dunno, *some* people are stupid enough to forget," said the boy.

"Don't call him stupid, Casey," said the girl with braided hair who'd said she was a healer. "He's dead. Show some respect."

"Any luck?" Helen whispered to me.

"No, but I didn't sense any lies," I whispered back. "I think I might need to talk to the sirens. My lie-sensing power doesn't work on speculation, only direct statements. And it's affected by whatever the person I'm talking to believes is the truth."

"Oh." Her face fell. "It's better than nothing, though, right? Casey is having a tough time with all the accusations. He and Terrence were on the same Sky Hopper team."

"Well, he didn't lie," I said. "It sounds like the sirens might have been involved, but I'd need to talk to them to be sure."

Which meant another trip to the lake. I didn't have time for that now… wait a moment. I got out my phone to check the time.

"I'm late for work," I said, backing towards the gates. "I'll see you later, Helen. Sorry."

I took off, switching on my Seven-Millimetre Boots with a click of the button on the heel. Gliding wasn't quite as effective as flying, but my fairy form came with the unfortunate side effect of shedding glitter everywhere. Showing up late at the office would be bad enough without adding a glitter shower on top of it.

I glided to a halt in front of the doors of Dritch & Co's

office, skidded inside, and sagged with relief when I spotted Callie behind her usual desk and the boss nowhere in sight.

"Hey, Blair." Callie waved at me. She was a friendly-faced blond woman who occasionally looked like a snarling wolf when I glanced at her out of my peripheral vision. My paranormal-sensing power had become background noise now, for the most part, but seeing a wolf in the corner of my eye in place of a pretty blond woman still weirded me out sometimes.

"Hey." I approached the door to the main office at the back. "I guess the boss is late aga—"

I broke off as the door swung inwards. Veronica Eldritch sat in my desk chair before a stack of paperwork, her silver-white hair splayed over the back of the seat.

"I'm glad you decided to join us, Blair." She slid to her feet with more poise than I could achieve even with my boots.

"Oh, sorry I'm late." I took my seat with as much dignity as I could muster. It was typical that Veronica would show up early the one day I lost track of time.

"What were you doing, exactly?" she enquired.

"Er, meeting with Helen," I said. "She's giving me broomstick lessons as part of my training."

"Well, try to do that outside of work hours next time. And you have a note from your friend Nathan." She pressed a piece of paper into my hand.

Oh, no. He must have come here and missed me. Weird that he hadn't texted instead—unless I'd missed that, too. I was in dire need of a shot of motivational coffee to wake up my brain.

"Okay, thanks. I'll make up the time after work."

"Do that." She left the office, at which point I made a beeline for the coffee machine and hit the button on the side for an extra-large motivational coffee. Then I checked

Nathan's note. It invited me to his house for dinner with his family this evening.

Apparently, it was one of those days. I took my coffee and returned to my seat, my stomach somersaulting with nerves. The chaos of the morning had wiped Nathan's family from my mind. *It's okay. It's only a family dinner, not a trial.*

Bethan raised her eyebrows at me. "Broomstick lessons? You?"

"If I'm to skip a grade, I have to at least know the basics," I said. "Didn't you hear what a spectacle I made of myself at the witches' place last night?"

"No," she said. "Why, did you hit yourself in the face with it?"

"Nope, I nearly knocked Helen out cold and made a fool of myself in front of a whole pack of schoolchildren *and* their parents."

Bethan laughed. "Only you, Blair."

"Oh, Helen," said Lizzie. "She seems nice. If a bit over-enthusiastic. If she wasn't married to the academy, I might consider asking her to apply here."

"Wait, are we hiring a fourth person again?" I blew on my coffee to cool it down.

"We are," Bethan confirmed. "This time, Mum wants us to interview them in person to make sure they're a good fit. To avoid a repeat of last time."

Our office didn't have the best track record for keeping employees. Firstly, Blythe had been fired for hexing both Callie and me in an attempt to get me kicked out. Then Lena had barely lasted a few weeks before she'd been hit by Rebecca's personality-altering powers and left town. The office was supposed to have four witches and some people—okay, Blythe—said it was bad luck to have anything less. I'd often thought *I* was the cause of the office's lingering streak of bad luck, but Dritch & Co had been having a great summer. At least since Veronica had been cleared of murdering someone who wasn't actually dead. Maybe we didn't need four witches to function, but it'd be even better if we weren't so over-worked all the time.

"Okay, who are the candidates?" I took a huge sip of coffee.

"Check the list," Lizzie said. "Veronica put you in charge since you did such a great job with the town's security team."

"Wait, she did?" I should be flattered, but I already had a full plate. For some reason, the universe always piled every-thing on me at once. "Right—we need a witch or wizard to keep with tradition, right? Or maybe we should branch out."

"I don't see anything wrong with branching out," Lizzie said. "Hiring a fairy didn't do us any harm. Maybe a vampire."

"Isn't one lie-detector enough for a single office?" I asked. "Pretty sure I referred all the newest vampires to the town security team, anyway. The older ones don't need to work since they're all millionaires."

"Werewolves?" Lizzie suggested.

"Chief Donovan still has us blacklisted," Bethan said. "We have Callie, besides. See who's on the list."

I checked the list of names atop the pile of papers on my desk. Mostly witches and wizards, by the look of things.

"A wizard?" I suggested. "Is there a reason we're witches only?"

"No, it just worked out that way," Bethan said. "There used to be a wizard here before me. Maybe we could give a few people a trial run to see if they're a good fit rather than just hiring the first person who applies. Uh, not that it didn't work out great in your case, Blair."

"Good idea," I said, scanning the details of each candidate. "People who can stand to be around chaos and who don't mind dealing with..." I trailed off, looking at the picture of a huge blond man at the top of the list. "Uh, what you said about were-wolves? How did Chief Donovan's nephew end up on the list?"

Bethan frowned. "He did?"

I turned the paper around to show her. "Veronica isn't under a spell again, is she?"

"No… Let's ask Callie."

She got to her feet and walked out of the office to find the blond receptionist. I followed close behind her.

"Hey, Callie," I said. "Did your cousin apply to work here? Robert?"

Her brow wrinkled. "Oh, no. Not again."

"Not again what?" I asked. "Is this the same cousin who nearly started a fight with me in the witches' place last month?"

"No. It's his brother, Rob." She glanced nervously at the boss's office. "I think he may have applied as a joke to annoy my dad. He's the rebellious cousin."

"And do you think he'd be a good fit here?" Lizzie asked, coming out of the open door behind us.

Callie gave another glance at Veronica's office before dropping her voice. "Maybe? But you know, my dad still hasn't lifted the ban on people from the pack applying here. I don't know how my cousin got around it."

"We don't want to annoy the pack," I said. "But you're still allowed to stay here, right, Callie?"

"He can't stop me from going to work," she said. "But… oh, no. She looked at her phone, which had buzzed on the desk. "He said he's coming here…"

The front doors slid open.

"…now," she finished.

A blond man walked through the doors into the reception area. "Hey, there," he said. "Which of you is Veronica Eldritch?"

"None of us." Bethan backed towards the open office door. "I'm her daughter. You applied for the position of our fourth team member, right?"

"Right." He gave Callie a wave and peered behind her desk. "Is that Ms Eldritch's office?"

"We're running the interviews," I said, certain Veronica wouldn't want her time wasted with someone who'd only applied as a joke. "In here."

He wasn't the same cousin who'd once yelled at me, at least, but let's just say the werewolf pack and I weren't best friends. If I tried to kick him out, things could get nasty, and I'd had more than enough close encounters with werewolf teeth for a lifetime. Instead, I'd have to employ my best techniques to be rid of him.

He strode into our office and waved at Lizzie. "Hey there," he said. "I've heard all about your magical printer. Was it you who repainted Francis's face?"

"Who?" I said blankly.

"The gargoyle who got covered in printer ink a few weeks ago," said Lizzie, looking as though she was trying not to laugh. "Aren't you going to interview him, Blair?"

"Uh, usually we pick who to invite for interviews first," I said pointedly. "Unless one of you two emailed him?"

There was an awkward pause, and Bethan cleared her throat.

"I was half asleep when I sent the email yesterday," Lizzie admitted. "I don't have your talent, Blair."

"Talent?" Rob said, sounding curious.

"Never mind." If nothing else, my lie-sensing power would clear up the issue of whether or not he actually wanted to be here. Then I'd have to find a tactful way to be rid of him before Chief Donovan showed up on the doorstep and demanded to know why I was hiring all his relatives. I'd wanted to avoid the pack for the foreseeable future, but it would be rude to turn him away.

I invited the werewolf into the small room we used for interviews, and then severely regretted it. He took up half the room, and the chair looked like a kids' chair when he sat on it. At least he didn't get into my personal space. When I'd first come here, I'd been terrified at the idea of conducting an interview with a werewolf alone in a cupboard-sized room, but now, all I hoped was that he wouldn't waste my time.

"So, I'm Rob," he said. "I'd love to work for Eldritch & Co."

True… but that didn't tell me *why*. "Tell me about the skills you have which would make you a good fit for our team," I said. "You may have noticed that all our staff except Callie are witches."

"They are? I didn't notice." He sat up straighter. "Skills. I'm good at scaring off trespassers."

Resisting the impulse to roll my eyes, I said, "I don't remember that being on the job requirements list."

"That's not all I can do," he said. "I assumed that after all the break-ins you've had this year, you'd want more hired muscle."

"We have the town's security to help us out if necessary," I said. "And Veronica's security wards are second to none. Do you have any admin experience?"

"Yeah, I ran the chess club at the university. I was also part of the cross-paranormal debate team."

"So you studied at the university. Which course?"

Rob leaned forward and the chair creaked alarmingly. "Yes, I have a degree in accounting. Did you not read my application form?"

No, because you showed up here without warning. I really needed more coffee. "Okay, you do meet our main requirements," I admitted. "If you were hired to select a candidate for a unicorn-handing position, what would you do?"

I launched into the 'hypothetical scenarios' section of the interview. I was pretty sure nobody was ever honest in that section, but not only did I pick up on zero lies from him, he answered every question perfectly.

In fact, he was the ideal candidate. If only he'd applied for genuine reasons and not to annoy someone I didn't want to make an enemy of.

"Where do you see yourself in five years?" I finished with the most annoying of all possible interview questions.

"Sitting in a hammock," he said, with a grin.

True. He'd got through the entire interview without lying, and I was officially out of ideas. "Okay, thanks for your time. I'll let you know if you get the job within the next five working days."

He gave me a cheery smile. "Sure. I look forward to it."

Rob left, while I rubbed my forehead, thoroughly annoyed with myself. The others stared at me when I walked back into the office.

"How'd it go?" Bethan asked.

I shook my head, disgruntled. "Looks like he's sincere about wanting to work here. I wish I'd just asked outright if he's trying to annoy Chief Donovan. Or if he just wants to work in an office full of witches only for the bragging rights."

The door to the reception opened, and Rob backtracked into the office. Oops. I'd thought he'd left. "Oh, Chief Donovan won't make trouble for you," he said. "Also, I didn't notice you were all witches when I applied, but I don't have nefarious intentions. I'm not interested in women."

And then he was gone. I waited a moment in case he came back, then said, "I shouldn't have said that."

"Look on the bright side," said Lizzie. "You don't have to

interview any of the other candidates. We have a fourth team member again."

"I wouldn't be so sure." I walked out into the reception area. "Is he gone, Callie?"

"Yes, he is." She frowned at me. "What in the world were you asking him? He was in there for ages."

I groaned. "I tried every line of questioning and he didn't slip up at all. He seems to actually want to be here. Was he serious?"

"I'm not the human lie detector."

"She's got you there," said Bethan from behind me.

I gave another sigh and walked back into the office. "That's what I get for conducting interviews before I finished my coffee." Which was now cold. I drank it down anyway, mentally kicking myself. If Chief Donovan and Veronica got into a duel in the office, the blame would fall squarely on my head.

"I didn't put two and two together with the name," Lizzie said. "But he actually seems a good fit."

"Uh, except for the part where Chief Donovan now has two relations working for his least favourite people in town?"

"Nah, we aren't his least favourite. Don't forget the vampires," said Bethan. "Besides, it's better than trying out witches who aren't used to our special brand of weirdness. Rob seems like a cool guy."

"Hmm." I drained the rest of my coffee and picked up the candidate list again. "I don't know. Chief Donovan still hasn't forgiven me for Callie falling under that spell. Not to mention... uh, I'm having dinner with Nathan's family tonight."

Bethan's jaw dropped. "You... what?"

"I'm meeting Nathan's family," I said. "Off duty. It's not a hunter thing. I don't think they'll be probing me about the town's issues or anything. Just if the werewolves hear about that…"

"Oh." Lizzie winced. "Yeah, I didn't know that when I emailed him. But he seems to fit in well here. He's certainly charismatic. We need more of that."

"We have plenty of charm." I shuffled the files. "What we don't have is someone to sit on the end of the phone when a problem client is on a roll and listen patiently without 'accidentally' hanging up."

"He could just growl at the problem clients and they'd give in," Bethan observed. "That's it, we're keeping him."

I sighed.

———

After another long afternoon of interviews, I left the office twenty minutes late, having made up the lost time for this morning. I'd just about have time to go home and change before heading to meet Nathan's family.

Nerves fluttered inside me. I'd barely been able to concentrate all afternoon, and maybe it was because of that, but none of the other possible candidates seemed the right fit for our office. Bethan and Lizzie were right: Rob was the best option out of all the interviewees. But the last thing I wanted was to open up a new line of conflict with the werewolves.

As it turned out, the werewolves weren't who I should have been worried about. I reached home to find a small figure wearing bark-coloured clothes standing on my doorstep. It was Bramble the elf.

"Oh, hi," I said, surprised. When the elves paid me a visit, the king usually sent one of his personal guards. I hadn't known Bramble knew where I lived. "Can I help you with something?"

"Probably not," he said.

Okay... "Er, not to be rude, but I'm on my way to dinner with my boyfriend's family. Can you come back later?"

"No," he growled. "The gargoyles are blaming us for that human's death."

"Oh, no." Steve dealt with criminal investigations with the finesse of a bucket of weed killer unleashed on a garden. I should have guessed he'd find someone to blame who hadn't been near the crime scene. Though I *had* seen the elves on the path by the falls, and I'd bet they hadn't been willing to play nice and answer the police's questions.

"Exactly," Bramble said. "You can vouch for us, can you not? Tell the gargoyle we weren't involved with the boy's death."

"I don't work with Steve," I said. "He doesn't even care about my lie-sensing power—he never believes a word I say. Why did he end up accusing you to begin with?"

There was a pause, then he said, "We were near the lake when that student drowned. Someone saw us in the woods."

"What were you doing by the falls?" I asked. "You don't normally come to the lake, do you?"

"What business is it of yours?" he said haughtily.

And he wondered why Steve had assumed him guilty. "I'm just trying to help. You *didn't* kill the guy, did you?" I had to get that straightened out first.

"Certainly *not*," he said. "None of my people murdered a human. How dare you even assume such a thing?"

"You just told me you were a suspect." Never mind a fourth team member—I needed a personal assistant with finesse in handling paranormal relations. "All right, I'll try to help, but I don't think Steve will listen to me."

"I will return to take you to our king later, human," he growled.

Then he stepped off the doorstep and disappeared into the nearby bushes.

What have I got myself into this time?

I let myself into the flat. Alissa wasn't in, so she wouldn't have seen the elf standing outside. I should probably count myself lucky that he hadn't shown up at the office.

I dropped off my bags and contemplated my wardrobe. What was I supposed to wear to a fancy dinner with Nathan's family? The hunters I'd met dressed like they were ready to go hiking most of the time. Still, it was best to make a good impression. I discarded a dozen outfits before settling on my nicest top and skirt. It was too warm for a cardigan or jacket. I changed quickly, then I applied some makeup in the bathroom mirror.

I put on a pleasant smile, a leftover from my customer service days, and surveyed my reflection. There. I looked normal. Perfectly human and normal.

"Miaow." Sky rubbed against my legs.

"Hey, Sky," I said. "I'm off to see Nathan's family. Wish me luck, huh?"

"Miaow," he said, which could have meant anything from *good luck* to *I hope he likes cats.*

"I'll be back in a bit, okay?" I checked my reflection one last time, hoping that Nathan's family wouldn't notice that all my clothes were covered in cat fur.

Go time. No pressure, Blair.

4

I walked halfway down the road, then stopped. Hang on… where was Nathan's house? I checked my phone. He'd texted me the address, which I ought to have already known. He lived up the north side of town, so I walked in that direction, past the vampires' cemetery, and turned right. I hoped I wasn't sweating too much. It was uncomfortably warm outside, and my nerves got worse with every step. I wished I could use my wings as a shortcut, but if I flew there in fairy form, I'd lose the image of a normal human I'd worked hard to cultivate.

Nathan's redbrick house was on a terraced street which looked almost like it belonged to a normal magic-free English town. Maybe he'd picked this location on purpose to give his family the impression that the whole town was just as harmless. His neighbours must surely be paranormals, since he was the only ex-hunter in town, but they seemed to be on their best behaviour. Granted, since they had the curtains drawn, they might be jousting on unicorns behind the scenes for all I knew. Nathan's living room curtains were open, however, and I glimpsed several people inside. My stomach tightened.

I took in a deep breath and knocked. Nathan answered the door wearing jeans and a T-shirt. Okay, maybe this wasn't as formal an event as I thought, but it didn't hurt to make a good impression.

"You look great, Blair," he said.

"Don't stand in the way, Nathan. Let me see her." A woman elbowed him aside. She had long dark hair and wore muddy jeans and a leather jacket that stretched across her muscular shoulders.

"Hey," she said, reaching out a hand to shake mine. "You must be Blair. I'm Erin. It's great to meet you. Nathan's told me so much about you."

"Ah, it's great to meet you, too," I said. All I knew about her was that she was trying to impress her family by being a hunter and she liked bubble wrap. And the outdoors, judging by the state of her clothes.

"You're not his usual type," Erin said to me. "I'm surprised."

From her tone, she was teasing, so I didn't take her bait. As I entered the narrow hallway, a tabby cat brushed against my legs. "Right, you have three cats." I crouched to stroke the cat behind its ears. "I remember you told me."

Erin gave him a curious look. "What, you haven't been to his place yet? How long have you been together?"

"Really, Erin," he said. "It's been a busy summer, what with my promotion and everything. Blair's busy, too, with work."

She grinned at me. "Right, you work for that weird woman with the white hair. Veronica Eldritch. Wasn't she married to that shifter who's been arrested twelve times for public nudity?"

Nathan frowned. "Erin, what did I tell you about spreading stories?"

She shrugged. "Just what I heard. Oh, hey, Eric."

A young man of around her age stepped out of the door behind her. He looked a little like Nathan, but he'd grown his dark brown hair to shoulder length and wore the same rugged gear as his sister.

"Hey," he said. "Jay is keeping Dad occupied… you must be Blair. Good to meet you."

"You too," I said, shaking his hand. "You're…"

"I'm Eric," he said. "Erin's twin."

"Oh, cool."

"Yeah, our parents ran out of ideas for names. They weren't expecting twins." Erin winked. "Of course that was also the year Mum took off, so—"

"Erin." Nathan pointedly indicated the slightly open door on the right. Then he pushed it open, revealing a spacious living room. "Blair's here."

I walked into the living room, where two men sat on the leather sofa. Nathan's dad had grey hair and wore casual clothes like Nathan rather than hiking gear. The younger man, however, wore dark brown clothes almost like army fatigues. I knew immediately that he was the oldest sibling, the one in charge of the local hunters' branch. If the clothes hadn't tipped me off, the knives strapped to his waist would have.

"*You're* Blair?" he said, rising to his feet. "Huh. I suppose you're pretty at least. Shame about everything else."

"Jay," Nathan said warningly.

Everything else? Really? He'd once described his siblings as 'thick as stumps' and similar to the other three hunters I'd met, so it came as no surprise that at least one of them would take an instant dislike to me. Still, it was awkward standing there while he looked me up and down as though hoping someone else would appear in my place.

"I'm Blair," I said. "Blair Wilkes. You're…"

"I'm Jay." He didn't offer to shake my hand.

"And I'm Mr Harker, Nathan's father," said the grey-haired man. He stood and shook my hand. He had a very firm grip. Strong. They all were. Erin looked like she could throw me through a window.

"It's great to meet you all," I said.

"And you, of course," Mr Harker said.

Lie.

Of all the times to have an inner lie detector. I wished I could put it on mute for the evening.

"Nathan told us a little about you," said Mr Harker.

"But we all want to hear more," said Erin, striding into the room. "Tell us, Blair."

"There's not much to tell," I said. The four of them staring at me was somehow worse than being laughed at by small children while falling off a broomstick.

"I think there is," said Nathan's father. "You're a witch, right? You're not with one of the local covens."

"Ah, I was adopted," I said. "My foster parents retired to Australia. They don't know about the paranormal world."

"And you're planning to tell them?" Mr Harker asked.

Huh? He must know it was illegal. Was this some sort of test?

"No," I said. "I've only lived here a few months."

"Well, you tamed Nathan in that time," put in Erin.

Nathan gave her a warning look. "I was actually the first person Blair met when she came here."

"Really?" Her eyes lit up. "Tell us all about it."

"It's not that interesting a story," I said. "I mean, I got lost on my way to a job interview. I thought I was applying to something in the normal world… long story. Anyway, I ran into Nathan at the town border by the lake."

"You didn't know?" asked Mr Harker. "How could you apply to a job here and not know it was a paranormal town?"

"Ah, it was a misunderstanding," I said hastily, wishing I'd never brought up the subject. "I had latent paranormal powers and showed up on a contact list for Eldritch & Co even though I didn't know this world existed."

"Is that common here in Fairy Falls?" asked Mr Harker.

Trying to get gossip for the hunters? Or just curiosity? I couldn't say.

"No," Nathan said. "But Blair's mother lived here, which is likely why her name came up when Veronica was searching for candidates. We don't have many outsiders come in, and even fewer people grow up in the normal world without knowing they're paranormal."

"Who cares? I'd rather get to know Blair personally," Erin interjected. "So, Blair, tell me about your first date with Nathan."

"Uh…" I somehow doubted Nathan's relatives wanted to hear about the time we'd had to run out of the pub during a date to confront the wand-maker who'd faked his own death, or the time I'd had to be escorted home by a bunch of over-enthusiastic security witches because he'd been called out to investigate a monster attack. "We just… went to the pub together. Nothing fancy."

"Not at all," Nathan said. "Blair, can you come and help me set the table?"

I escaped the room gratefully, pursued by two small tabby cats.

"Cute," I said, scratching one of them behind the ears. "What're their names?"

"That's Whiskers and Patches. Maurice is hiding upstairs. He doesn't like noise."

"Ah." I walked after him into the dining room, where the table was laid out. "I didn't know you cooked."

"I had to learn to take care of my younger siblings," he said. "Anyway—what is your cat doing here?"

"My what?"

I looked where he pointed. Sure enough, Sky sat up at the table, paws resting on the tablecloth as though waiting for me to notice him. When I'd seen him out of the corner of my eye, I'd assumed he was one of Nathan's cats, but that eye colour combination wasn't a common one.

"Sky… what are you doing here?" Had he taken me seriously when I'd suggested he show up to meet Nathan's family?

"Miaow."

I walked behind him. "Sky, this is a family dinner."

"Oh, he's *adorable!*" Erin squealed, bouncing into the room. "Is he yours, Blair?"

"I think he followed me here." I made to pick him up, and he jumped off the seat and ran towards Erin. *Traitor.*

Erin stroked him behind the ears. Sky purred and bounded onto the table. A glass wobbled, and I lunged to catch it.

"I'm sorry," I said to Nathan, setting the glass down. "I can send him home—"

"Oh, don't worry," said Erin, picking him up. "Nathan's cats will never let me pick them up like this."

"He doesn't normally let *me* do that," I said, feeling my normal-human act begin to collapse. *Why me?*

"Miaow," said Sky, and purred.

"Hey, Eric!" Erin called. "Meet Blair's cat."

At least they'd stopped asking me awkward questions— but what was Sky playing at?

Eric came into the room. "Hey. How'd he get in?"

"Probably the cat flap." Saying *he appeared from nowhere* would not help me pretend both of us were totally normal.

"He has such unusual eyes!" Erin said. "What breed is he, do you know?"

"I don't," I lied. "He's adopted. Well, he adopted me."

"Aww," she said. "Tell me the story."

"It was my first week in town, and he followed me home from the bookshop. I think he was a stray for a while." Though he'd been friends with the leader of the local vampires—not that they needed to know that. "He just saw me and that was it. I was his owner."

"That's so cute!" Erin said. "Cats know what they want, don't they?"

"Miaow," said Sky.

"He's a familiar, right?" she asked. "That means he's magical."

"Uh, kind of."

I'd bet Nathan hadn't told them I was half fairy, much less the unusual nature of my cat. I wished I'd made an excuse and stayed at home rather than tempting fate.

Jay walked into the room, and Sky hissed at him. He started. "Whose cat is that?"

"My cat followed me," I explained. "This is Sky. Sky, meet—"

Sky jumped out of Erin's arms and dove under the table.

"He can sometimes be weird around strangers." Never mind that Sky's default mode was 'weird'—I needed to get him out of here before Nathan's dad came in.

I crouched down. "Hey, Sky, come out. It's okay."

"What in the world is that?" Jay said loudly.

I jumped, hitting my head on the table. Stars winked before my eyes and I withdrew my head to see the pixie hovering outside the window, surrounded by a cloud of glitter. Oh, *no*.

"Is that glitter?" Jay said. "Where's it coming from?"

You have got to be kidding me. They couldn't see the pixie, so it looked like glitter had appeared from thin air. Nathan looked at me and I gave a helpless shrug.

The pixie tapped on the window. I shook my head at him, trying to indicate that now wasn't the best time. He ignored my head-shake and rapped against the glass, louder. Everyone looked around for the source of the noise, but the pixie remained hidden by glamour only I could see through.

Go away, pixie. Now is not *the time.* I shook my head yet again, and this time the pixie vanished.

Then he reappeared inside the room—above the dining table. I looked at him in utter horror. *Please, no.*

"Blair, is something wrong?" asked Erin.

"Nope." The pixie flew higher, its tiny wings beating like a hummingbird's. I hadn't a hope of catching it and tossing it outside, especially with everyone watching me.

Erin crouched down and beckoned to Sky to come out from under the table. "Hey, Sky… Blair, where did your cat go? He's not here."

I could hazard a guess: he'd gone out the same way he'd come in—by vanishing. I'd much rather deal with the cat than a hyper, glitter-shedding pixie. Just what was he doing here?"

"He must have run out," I said.

"He's a magical cat, right?" Erin said.

"Uh, yeah." I looked up at the ceiling as though I could make the pixie disappear by sheer force of will. "He has a very strong personality." And I had a very strong desire to run for the hills.

"Why is there glitter on the table?" asked Jay.

"There isn't." There was. The pixie had also dropped glitter on Jay's head. Nathan's eyes went wide.

Drawing my wand right now would not be wise, but I

could glamour something invisible. Okay, I'd only practised on myself---unless you counted the time I'd accidentally turned Sky invisible—but I had to do something.

I clenched my right hand at my side and snapped my fingers as quietly as possible.

Vanish, I thought urgently. *Vanish—*

The table disappeared.

Oh, no. Somehow, I'd managed to glamour the table... and everything on it.

"De-glamour," I muttered, snapping my fingers. If I wasn't careful, I'd de-glamour myself, which was *not* what I needed. I tried again. This time, everyone looked at me.

"Blair, did you do that?" Erin asked, her brow furrowing.

"I'm sorry," I said. "I was trying to get rid of the glitter. I'll fix it." I snapped my fingers frantically, but the table stayed invisible. Maybe I should try my wand instead. I pulled it from my pocket and streamers of blue light shot from the end. The others jumped out of the way, knocking into the invisible table. I heard a glass fall to the floor and winced at the sound.

"Sorry!" I put the wand away and snapped the fingers of my right hand. *De-glamour. De-glamour!*

"Are you going to get rid of this?" said Jay, who had bright streamers all over his head and glitter in his hair. It'd have been hilarious if I wasn't so utterly horror-struck.

"Give me a second!" I kept snapping my fingers, wishing I could glamour myself invisible and run off instead. But it wouldn't be fair to leave Nathan to deal with the fallout.

Finally, the table reappeared, glitter and all. Most of the glasses had fallen over and everything was covered in purple sparkles.

Then the doorbell rang. I ignored it and pulled out my wand to get rid of the glitter. To my intense relief, the vanishing spell worked.

Nathan peered out the window. "It's for you, Blair."

"Huh? Nobody saw me come here." The pixie being an obvious exception. Then again, it might be best for everyone if I left.

I strode to the window and looked outside. Two elves stood on the doorstep. You might know it.

The doorbell rang again. Nathan gave me a questioning look, and what was left of my resolve unravelled like an old jumper. "Sorry. I'll get it."

I hurried from the room, my face flushed past 'embarrassed' and more in the category of 'please sign me up for the next mission to the moon, never to return again'.

Opening the door a fraction, I whispered, "What are you doing here?"

"Blair Wilkes," said Bramble. "The king would like to see you."

"I'm sorry, we're in the middle of an important family dinner at the moment," I said. "Can you come back later?"

How had they known I was here? They must have followed the pixie. He and I would be having serious words later.

"This *is* later," Bramble growled. "No humans are as important as the king's request."

"I have to disagree with you there," I said, conscious that the others had come into the hall behind me to witness my awkward conversation through the crack in the door. "Also, I *am* human."

"I beg to differ." The elf snapped his fingers. I jumped backwards, and my wings brushed the walls.

My wings. Oh *no*.

I properly opened the door, giving the elves a glare. "What do you think you're playing at?"

"The king would prefer you to visit wearing your real form."

"Right." Perfect. Nathan's family stood directly behind me, staring in disbelief at my glittery wings. Never mind the moon. I'd board the next spaceship to the most distant corner of the galaxy possible if it got me out of here, right now.

"Blair, maybe you should go and see what your friends want," Nathan said.

"They're not my friends."

"How dare you!" Bramble said. "You are a friend of the king's and you *will* do as we tell you."

I cast Nathan an apologetic look. "Okay, I'll deal with it. I'm sorry."

If it was possible to die of humiliation, I'd be on my way to the morgue, not to visit the elf king. Had I accidentally put a dash of lucky latte in my coffee yesterday and run headlong into the backlash?

"What in the world was that for?" I said to the elves when we were out of earshot of the house. "I'm supposed to be meeting my boyfriend's family and thanks to you and the pixie, they think I'm a raving lunatic."

"The pixie is your responsibility, not ours."

"He brought you here!" How much more could a person endure in a single day? "Not to be rude, but I don't work for you or the king. You just got me into a lot of trouble."

"You told us you would help," growled Bramble. "I thought you kept your word."

"I will, but seriously, this is out of order." I kept walking after them. The forest wasn't far off, but in this part of town, most of it would be elf territory. "So you want me to defend you against Steve?"

"The king is very concerned about the accusations levelled against Twig and myself, as well as Bracken," Bramble said.

"Bracken? Is he the elf who was drunk by the waterfall, by

any chance?" He'd also looked familiar. I *had* seen him before. A few months ago, I'd seen him meeting Annabel Reece, the seer's granddaughter, in the woods. The two had been dating, and as far as I knew, were happy together. So why was he drunkenly staggering around by the lake and throwing insults at any humans who walked past?

"He is unable to defend himself against the accusations," said the other elf, who must be called Twig. Really imaginative names, the elves had. "But he is not a killer."

"Hmm." He wasn't lying, though it was hard to tell with the elves. Sometimes they acted in ways I could understand, and sometimes they sent pixies to crash dinner parties.

But despite that, I was kind of curious about who'd reported the elves to the police. Most likely, someone else had seen Bracken hanging around by the falls. He'd also called me *human filth,* which didn't sound like an insult someone who was dating a human would use. Maybe he and Annabel had broken up. But had he been involved with Terrence's death?

"Also," Bramble added, "the king has new information on your family that he thinks you'll want to know. He will give it to you on the condition that you tell the police that none of us committed the crime."

I knew there was another catch somewhere.

5

The elf king waited for me inside the hollow tree that served as the elves' lair. As usual, I had to half-lie, half-crouch, because the place was designed for four-foot-tall elves and not for five-foot-something humans with a giant pair of glittering fairy wings. It'd been the elf king who'd clued me in that my dad had sheltered from the hunters in the woods before his arrest, which meant I couldn't exactly write off his invitation, but his timing couldn't have been worse if he'd shown up to a funeral in a tutu.

"You have more information on my family?" I asked.

"I do," he confirmed, without elaborating.

"And you'll tell me if I talk to the police." I'd almost rather relive this evening's events than go within a mile of the gargoyle. Steve and Nathan weren't on friendly terms at the moment, so I wouldn't be able to bring him with me for moral support. Besides, he'd be occupied entertaining his family all week.

Just thinking about them brought a hot rush of shame. I'd been under no illusions that nothing would go wrong at all, since nobody could come to a paranormal town without expecting to encounter a little magical chaos. But I hadn't expected things to go *that* far out of control. I had to see this through or I'd have endured the humiliation for nothing.

"I will," he said. "I would not want any of my own to end up jailed for a crime they didn't commit."

"Uh, if you don't mind my asking, what were your people doing by the falls to begin with?" I asked. "I'll need to give the police their alibi if someone saw them near the crime scene. It's the only way Steve might listen to me."

Bramble scowled. "We own the forest. We're entitled to walk in it."

All right, then. "What kind of information on my family are we talking about? More about my dad?"

Why had he broken contact with me? Did he think I was in mortal danger if I stayed here? If he did, I would have expected *more* correspondence from him, not less. I didn't even see the pixie much anymore. Except, of course, when I tried to pretend to be normal in front of my boyfriend's family.

My dad had believed his life was in danger when he'd fled to the forest and that mine would be in danger, too, if I stayed in the paranormal world. The only explanation I could think of for his more recent panic was that he'd found out Inquisitor Hare, leader of the hunters, had invited me to join them. In fairness, it'd freaked me out too, but he hadn't been in town since I'd turned his offer down. I didn't see how my dad could possibly have found out about his offer unless the pixie had told him.

"Have you heard from any of my other family members?" I pressed, when the elf king didn't answer. "Or has my dad told you why he's in jail?"

"Maybe."

I suppressed a groan. "Please, can you just be straight

with me? And, er, next time you urgently need to talk to me, can you send me a note or pick a time when I can afford to be interrupted by a glitter-wielding pixie?"

"If you do not give us instructions, how can we know?" Bramble said. "You told us to come back later."

"That wasn't—" I broke off. Clearly, elves didn't operate by the same rules as humans did. "Okay, I'll try to help you. But I don't think I can convince Steve. Like I said, I don't work for the police and I'm not a detective. Steve kind of hates my guts, actually."

"You made a promise, Blair Wilkes," the king said. "See to it that you keep it."

The dismissal was clear. I left the cave, pursued by the certain knowledge that the elves might inflict a worse humiliation on me than a glitter-wielding pixie if I turned my back on the case.

Talking to Steve wouldn't be pretty, though. He and Nathan were barely on speaking terms and the only reason they hadn't kicked off a major argument over the last couple of weeks was because they'd left one another to do their own thing. On the other hand, it didn't have to be Steve I spoke to. I could try one of the other gargoyles. The receptionist didn't hate me, but she wasn't one of the gargoyles with the power to give someone a life sentence on a whim.

I'd made a promise. Now I had to keep it.

I walked down the woodland path, then beat my wings and took to the air. While the gargoyles had trouble fitting their huge leathery wings down the narrow paths, my wings were as thin as net curtains and wove among the trees as easily as the pixie did when it fluttered around the house. My limbs occasionally smacked into a tree when I went too fast, but I had to admit I was much more coordinated in this form than I was as a human. Perhaps my clumsiness came from my glamour, the same way my propensity for accidentally destroying technology in the normal world had come from the spell hiding that I was paranormal even from myself.

Maybe the harder I denied what I was, the more likely it was to come spilling out. Who was I kidding, thinking I could have a nice normal dinner with my boyfriend's straight-laced family? Pushing my magical nature under the table was like trying to ignore a house fire.

After a few minutes, I found myself in a part of the woods I recognised, not far from the lake. I'd been here before a couple of months ago when Alissa and I had been trying to solve the murder of a pirate wizard's ghost, killed by his siren girlfriend. Dating a paranormal who could sing until you drowned was hazardous, to say the least. Might something similar have killed Terrence? Even if it hadn't been malicious, sirens' magic was known to be deadly and Terrence hadn't exactly been at his most observant.

I stopped walking, spotting the lake glistening through the trees. Since I was here, it was worth getting the sirens' version of the story, not to mention it'd be a welcome distraction from my disastrous evening.

The sirens rarely swam in the shallows, preferring deeper water. They were also reputed to be unpredictable, not to mention crafty, so messing with drunken students seemed right up their alley. I walked right to the edge of the water but didn't see any signs of life.

All right, I'd check by the falls. They seemed to like that area. I was still in fairy mode, so flying down to the river was simple enough. Aside from the crash of the waterfall, the small cave was deceptively peaceful-looking. Flecks of glitter splashed my skin from the falls. The spray could temporarily undo fairy glamour. Sirens could use glamour, too so perhaps they were hiding.

"Hey," I called out. "Are there any sirens here?"

I flew over the river, which widened as it merged with the

lake. Had Terrence drowned in here, or had his body washed into the cave from the lake?

I jumped in mid-air when a head popped up next to me. Unlike the blue-haired merpeople, the sirens looked close to human—albeit inhumanly beautiful. This one was no exception. Her glossy black hair fell around her face, and her skin was clear as porcelain without the wax-like quality vampires had. "Oh, hello," she said. "You're the fairy girl, right?"

"Uh, I guess I am." I *looked* like a fairy now, after all. "Can I talk to you?"

She pulled a face and dove underneath the water.

"Hey!" I said. "Wait, don't go."

Her head emerged again. "What do you want?"

"I just wanted to ask you a couple of questions. That's all. Did you see what happened here the other day? When Terrence drowned?"

"Are you with the human police?" She kicked up and down in the water, her hair fanning out in dark waves.

"Not exactly," I said. "But I heard Terrence might have spoken to one of you before he died. Did you know him?"

"Not well." She kicked onto her back. Sirens didn't wear much clothing, and her sheer dress showed me far more than I wanted to see. "He was fun."

Was she the siren Terrence's classmates had said he'd been flirting with?

"Did you see him the day he died?"

"Mm."

I'd need a more concrete answer if I was to get my inner lie detector to work. "I heard he had an argument with his classmate over going to swim with you, or something."

"Humans and their odd arguments." She flipped her hair. "I liked him. He made me laugh. I did speak to him the day he died. I told him I'd meet him at the shore when the others were gone."

Truth.

"Did you use your song on him?" I asked.

She shook her head. "No. I didn't want to bewitch him. I wanted a friend."

She's not lying. But there was some distinct discomfort in her tone that suggested she wasn't telling the whole truth.

"Did someone push him into the water?" I asked.

The siren flipped over, splashing me in the process. "No, I think he fell in. Humans are clumsy like that."

That didn't tell me much. Even if he'd lost his balance, there was his water-controlling power to consider.

"Doesn't your song cause wizards to lose their senses?"

"Yes." A spray rose as she kicked her feet, her expression agitated. "But I didn't use it on him. I like the academy humans."

True. But I'd been fooled by a siren before. One of them had even got around my lie-sensing power when she'd used her song to sneakily put it on mute. There wasn't any real way to counter a siren's song either unless I got my hands on another item similar to the harp that the pirate ghost had. He'd had to procure it so he could listen to his girlfriend's song without diving to his death in the water and it hadn't worked out well for him in the end, anyway.

The siren swam into the cave. "He was found here, right? Maybe he got tangled in the weeds."

"Hmm." I flew as close to the water as I dared and plunged my hand into it. The weeds weren't thick here, but he might have drowned further out into the lake and washed into the cave.

Or someone had moved his body into the cave to hide it and throw the police off the trail.

A flash of glitter caught my eye. I flew closer to the falls, frowning. That wasn't the spray of the water, but something solid and glassy. A bottle. Specifically, an empty wine bottle.

Another glint came from behind the spraying water. I tilted my head, squinting through the falls. Was there a cave *behind* the waterfall?

I sucked in a breath before ducking my head underneath the falls, reaching for the cave—and a hand grabbed me by the neck, throwing me under the water.

I thrashed, alarmed by the sudden attack. My head broke the surface of the water and I gasped for breath, flailing to grab the nearest surface. My hands grasped the bank and I pulled myself upright. Blinking water from my eyes, I twisted around and found myself face to face with the drunken elf I'd seen before. He leaned out of the cave behind the waterfall, oblivious to the glittery water raining down on his head.

"What are you doing?" I spluttered, spitting out water. "Did you just try to drown me?"

Bracken the elf squinted at me. "No. Did you try to touch my bottles?"

From the side view, I could distinctly see the small cave, where a small mountain of wine bottles lay beside the elf.

"I didn't know they were there," I protested. "Do you normally attack people who try to take your possessions from under the falls?"

He hiccoughed and didn't answer. I pulled myself onto the bank, shedding glitter in the process.

"Why are you here?" I asked him. Caution urged me to tread carefully. If he'd lash out and try to drown me, maybe he'd done the same to Terrence. His grip had been surprisingly strong considering the state of him, and maybe even a water wizard would have trouble fighting against the sheer thunderous power of the waterfall.

He ducked his head back into the cave. I coughed, glancing around. The siren had disappeared. She must have swum off. Not that I blamed her.

"You're the fairy," Bracken said from behind the falls. "Blair, the fairy."

"Yeah, why not. And I know you're called Bracken." I sat down on the bank, debating, then asked, "Were you trying to drown me?"

"I didn't try to drown you," he said, his voice muffled behind the water's spray.

"It sure looked that way." I shook out my damp hair. Even my wings were soaked through, and glitter sprayed the shore when I moved. "You dragged me under the falls. Did you do the same to someone else on Sunday?"

"No, no!"

True. "If you didn't do it, you were by the waterfall, right? Did you see what happened to Terrence?"

"Who?" he said.

"Academy student," I told him. "He drowned here in the lake on Sunday. The police are looking for leads and they're accusing two of your people because you were so close to the water. Did you see?"

He leaned through the waterfall again, the falls drenching his longish dark hair. "I wasn't here."

"Come on, you know that's not true," I said. "I *saw* you on the path. You called me a filthy human when I tried to stop you falling into the lake."

He blinked a couple of times, his gaze clouded. "I don't... remember."

Truth. Though maybe it didn't count. I wasn't sure if my lie detecting ability worked when the person in question didn't actually remember anything. I'd yet to test that one.

"Do you remember seeing any other people that day when you came to the falls?"

"No." Without warning, he collapsed in tears, the sound of loud sobbing rising alongside the crashing falls. Then he jumped through the falls, into the water. I worried for a moment that he'd drown *himself,* but he emerged a second later, dripping wet, and swam to join me on the shore.

"You said some unpleasant things about humans," I reminded him. "When I ran into you. Do you really not remember any of it?"

"No." He howled. "I hated her for ditching me. I don't even remember how I got here."

"Who's 'her'?" I asked. "Who are you upset with? Is it Annabel?"

He howled again at the sound of her name. "Yes, yes, beautiful Annabel. She broke off my heart, and nobody cares!"

"What about the other elves?" I said. "They were here too, weren't they?"

He sniffed again. "Yes, they're threatening to haul me back to the king in person. I don't want to go back there. I quit." He set his jaw defiantly.

"The king is concerned about you," I said, alarmed at his sudden outburst. "So are your friends, Bramble and Twig. Bracken, did you know the police are blaming you and the others for Terrence's death? He drowned in the falls, right here. Are you positive you didn't see anything?"

"I don't *remember.*" He slid back into the water and dunked his head under the falls again.

True. He wasn't lying, but I'd have to wait until he sobered up to get any more sense out of him.

"Are you sure?" I raised my voice over the crash of the falls. "Did you see any other people around here that day? In the water or otherwise?"

His head emerged. "I saw a lot of humans. I remember some on broomsticks…"

"The High Fliers." They'd still been in the sky when the academy students had finished their game. And they had a good view of the lake from up in the air. Maybe one of them had seen what'd happened.

The High Fliers would have to wait. When I flew out of the cave and back to the forest, rain had begun to fall, washing the glitter from my skin. I wasn't up for flying in the rain, and besides, it was getting late.

Time to go home... which meant facing the utter chaos I'd left behind. Maybe squatting in a cave behind a waterfall wasn't such a bad life plan after all.

***

"Oh, Blair," said Alissa, shaking her head at me. "You don't do things by halves, do you?"

"You're telling me." I buried my head in a cushion on the sofa. "Nathan hasn't even texted me since I disappeared, and I don't blame him. I thoroughly screwed up."

I'd spent the last half-hour explaining my nightmare of an evening. Alissa insisted on ordering takeout and we sat eating pizza on the sofa, accompanied by the cats.

"Miaow," was Sky's contribution to the discussion.

"It's all right for some people," I told him. "You're a cat. You can just disappear from awkward situations without anyone asking questions."

"He didn't like Nathan's family, then?" Alissa bit into her second slice of pizza.

"He didn't like his older brother, Jay." I lifted my head from the cushion and grabbed another slice. "He seemed fine with his other siblings. But he usually understands that some events are humans-only. I don't get why he was just—there."

"Maybe he thought you were inviting him."

"That's no reason for the pixie to take up an imaginary invitation, too." I chewed a mouthful of pizza. "He covered everything in glitter, *including* Nathan's family. Then the elves yanked me into the forest. It's my own fault. I said I'd go with them and I didn't specify *when,* so they picked the worst possible time by default."

"Ah," she said, wiping her fingers on a napkin. "I'd be *really* specific with them next time."

"Not sure there'll be a next time," I said. "Nathan's family thinks I'm a freak, and the elf king is dead set on me defending his drunken friend to Steve the bloody Gargoyle. Did someone spike my drink with a lucky latte?"

"Nope, it's just you, Blair."

"Wonderful. And on top of that, I nearly drowned." I explained my ill-fated encounter with the elf behind the waterfall.

"He tried to drown you?" Her eyes widened. "Okay, that doesn't seem like an innocent man, heartbroken or not."

"I know," I said. "Believe me. But if I don't prove to Steve that the elves didn't do it, then they won't tell me about my family. Again."

"That's blackmail." Alissa sipped from a glass of wine she'd brought out—not of the elf variety. "I know the elves don't follow human rules, but... do you think he committed the crime?"

"He doesn't remember," I said. "And the other two won't admit anything. I don't think *they* did it, but my lie-sensing power doesn't work as effectively if I'm dealing with someone who has no memory of what they did and why."

"I guess it's hard to defend someone with no memory," Alissa observed. "It also seems a weird place to hide, behind the Fairy Falls."

"You're telling me," I said. "He was hiding from the other elves, heartbroken because he was dating a human and she ditched him. Not sure why. I wouldn't think most people would then snap and murder a stranger, but he was completely addled and ranting against humans the day Terrence died."

"Ah," she said. "Who was he dating, do you know?"

"Annabel, the seer's granddaughter," I said. "You know, the one I accused of cursing Mr Falconer's apprentices. He's the reason she quit that apprenticeship, actually, so I thought they were serious. Not sure she'll want to speak to me, but it's her or Steve the gargoyle. Who knows, maybe she can coax a confession out of him."

Not that it'd make my relationship with the elves any less fractious, especially if it turned out he *was* guilty. The elves hadn't said what they'd do if that was the case, but I doubted it would involve them telling me the latest news on my family.

"Maybe," she said. "I'd tell you to leave the elves alone, but..."

"But they know my family," I finished. "And since *Nathan's* family hates me, at this rate, the fairies will be all I have left."

6

The following morning, Sky woke me up by licking my face. My first instinct was to look out the window for any signs of the pixie or the elves, but knowing my luck, they'd leave me alone until the next time I tried to meet with Nathan's family. Assuming there *was* a next time.

"Why me, Sky?" I said aloud.

"Miaow." His tone suggested he meant to say *get a grip, Blair.* Or he wanted me to feed him.

It wasn't all bad news. I was pretty sure the siren was innocent and less sure on the elves. It was still raining, so unless it cleared up by the time I got out of the office, talking to the High Fliers was out. At this stage, the best thing to do would be to talk to Annabel. She might not be my biggest fan, but she'd quit her apprenticeship to be with Bracken and from his reaction, whatever had caused their breakup must have been serious.

On the other hand, she had *not* been thrilled with me the last time I'd caused the police to haul her in for questioning. When I'd been investigating the curse on the wand-maker's apprentices, Annabel had been the natural suspect after I'd found out her grandmother and the wand-maker had argued shortly before the accident that had caused permanent magical damage to the old seer's mind. I'd later learned that she'd been the wand-maker's apprentice herself for all of a week until her relationship with the elf had led her to break it off. She'd been lucky, because if she'd stayed any longer, she'd have been turned into a mouse along with the other apprentices. While I'd helped solve that particular dilemma, Annabel had enough awareness of my lie-sensing power to be able to get around it if she wanted to and wouldn't be pleased that someone else she cared about might be implicated in a crime.

First, I had to get through work. I wished I hadn't told the others I'd be meeting Nathan's family. Where was a spell which erased humiliating events from existence when you needed one? You'd think the magical world would have come up with a solution. At least Alissa had left me a mug of extra-strength coffee before her shift. While I drank it, Sky followed me around, meowing.

"If you follow me to work, we're going to have to have words," I said to him. "Look, you never had any trouble staying at home before. What's the issue?"

He brushed himself against my legs again. I downed the rest of the coffee and gave him another stroke. "I already fed you," I said. "Stay put, Sky. I'll be back soon."

Sky swatted at Roald, Alissa's cat, who'd come to see what was going on.

"None of that either," I said sternly. "Sky, behave yourself."

Fairy cats. Honestly.

No elves ambushed me on the way to work. I made a point of leaving ten minutes early this time, but I was still the last to arrive at the office after I'd had to detach Sky from my legs four times on the way out the door.

Our little office bustled with activity. Lizzie, printing something, Bethan, going through files, Rob the werewolf... wait a minute. He wasn't supposed to be here. But Rob sat at the fourth unoccupied desk, for all the world as though he'd already been hired. "Er, Rob, what are you doing here?"

"I work here," he said. "Hey, Blair, it's great to see you."

"Okay..." I turned to Bethan for answers. "Wasn't I supposed to be interviewing other possible team members today?" Okay, the others I'd interviewed yesterday had left much to be desired, but still.

"You can get on with that while he helps out," said Bethan. "My mum's idea, but you're the one who suggested a trial shift."

So I had. "Um, Rob, does your uncle know you're here?"

He blinked his blue eyes. "I didn't know I was supposed to tell him whenever I went anywhere."

"I, uh, just wanted to make sure he won't get mad at us for hiring you," I explained. "Since he kind of blames me for the times Callie got stuck in wolf form, among other things. Let's just say we run into crises fairly often here."

"Oh." His face cleared. "You think I've never dealt with a crisis? I live in a pack where everyone turns into animals for several nights a month and spends the rest of the time playing in a band that sounds like a pixie got stuck in a blender."

Bethan and Lizzie both snickered with laughter. *So he doesn't like their music, either.* That put him higher in my estimation than most of the other werewolves I'd met.

"I'm not just here to annoy Chief Donovan," Rob said. "Trust me."

All right, then. At least his arrival should distract the others from asking me about my dinner with Nathan's family. Now if only I could avoid the subject for the next few decades, things would be just fine.

———

It was impossible to focus on interviewing other potential candidates with the werewolf's loud and boisterous presence behind me in the office. Half of them seemed to think he worked here already, and by the time I'd dismissed the final recruit, I was frazzled beyond measure.

"No new referrals," I muttered, returning to the office to find that everyone had already gone home. I walked to my desk, my heart swooping when I spotted a note. Not from Nathan, but Rob.

I tidied your desk, it said.

I looked at the teetering pile of papers, which had been divided into three more manageable stacks and seemed to be colour-coordinated, too. *Really?* I guess he was trying to get in my good books. I knew when I was beaten. Just as long as the chief of the werewolves didn't show up baring his teeth on my doorstep—or, god forbid, force me to watch his relatives perform in their band again—I was content to wash my hands of the matter. If the Chief had a problem with it... well, that was Veronica's problem, not mine.

I didn't have a magic lesson after work that day, so I made my way to Annabel's house, hoping that my latest streak of bad luck was behind me. The seer's granddaughter lived in a neat little cottage down the road from the main entrance to the witches' area of the forest. The trees grew close enough to her garden that I half expected to see blinking elf-eyes watching from the shadows, but nobody accosted me.

I knocked on Annabel's door. There was a long pause before she answered.

Annabel looked rough. Her fair hair was tangled around her heart-shaped face, and her grey-blue eyes were red-rimmed. "You again? What has my grandmother done this time?"

"Nothing," I said. "It's not about her. I know it's none of my business, but I ran into Bracken by the waterfall and he seemed pretty upset. He's drinking and acting erratically, and he said it's because you broke things off."

Annabel's gaze dropped. "I guess I did. End things. I mean. What's he doing by the waterfall?"

"Drinking himself into an early grave," I said. "It sounds like he's exiled himself from the elf community at large and has shut himself away in a cave behind the falls."

"Oh, for…" Her forehead screwed up. "I knew he'd over-react. What were you even doing by the falls? Wait, it's a fairy thing, isn't it? I don't want to know, then."

Her irritated tone signalled that not only did she have no idea what he was doing by the falls, but she didn't know about the murder accusation either.

"I was minding my own business when he grabbed me and nearly drowned me in the river because he thought I was going to steal his wine bottles." Partly true. Mostly, I wanted to see her reaction.

Her eyes brimmed over, and she shook her head. "The idiot isn't thinking clearly. I knew he'd do something stupid."

"Is there a reason you ended it?" I asked. "He implied it came out of nowhere."

"Why did I end it?" She blinked tears from her eyes. "Because I saw it."

"You saw what?" I asked, perplexed.

"I saw it. In a vision. I saw our relationship ending so I

decided to get ahead of fate and finish things before he could."

I frowned. "Your psychic powers showed a vision of you breaking up, so you made it happen?"

"Yes, that's what I said."

Hang on. "Uh… I thought you didn't have the seeing ability." Too late, I remembered I wasn't supposed to know that. I'd found out about her lack of talent when I'd been looking for clues as to whether she or her grandmother had cursed Mr Falconer's apprentices. Still, that'd been months ago, and she'd probably forgotten the details of our last conversation.

Her eyes clouded. "Yes. I didn't have the gift. But I started trying to use my grandmother's old crystal ball again, and since then, I've been having visions."

"Oh?" I said. "How do you know it's seeing? I mean… I don't know how it works, but I thought you could only develop magic in childhood." Unless it was suppressed like mine had been.

"So did I. My grandmother tried to teach me when I was younger," she said. "She kept trying, and I was always disappointed I didn't have the gift. But—now I do."

"But what if your vision was wrong? Isn't seeing… I'm not an expert, but I didn't think it was the most precise form of magic." Not according to Madame Grey or Rita anyway. 'Wishy-washy nonsense', Madame Grey had called it.

"I think seeing my relationship going up in flames was fairly clear." A tear dripped from her eye. "I had to finish things or else he'd have ended it anyway."

I got the impression that she wasn't in the mood to argue, but from what I'd heard from her grandmother, most seers' predictions were inaccurate, or in old Ava's case, totally made-up. Besides, a vision didn't seem worth wrecking a relationship over.

"Okay, help me understand," I said. "What happens if you

see something in a vision and let it play out? Does it always work like that, every time?"

"It's not always clear," she said. "Or strong. But I saw the two of us breaking up. There was no doubt about it."

"But did you have reason to think he might end it?" I asked.

She sniffed. "Well, no. Things were going great. Perfect, even. I thought we were going—going to get married. But the visions don't lie."

"Okay," I said. "Um, have you seen him since then?"

"What does it matter?" she snapped. "It's over. Why are you so interested, anyway?"

Here we go. "I don't know if you heard, but someone drowned in the lake last weekend. The police are giving the elves a hard time because he and a few of the others were seen near the lake right beforehand. He's claiming he was too drunk to remember anything that happened that day, but you know what Steve's like."

"Steve?" Her eyes widened. "Has Bracken been arrested?"

"Not yet, but I heard he's on the suspect list." Maybe they hadn't found him yet. The cave was pretty well-hidden.

"I can't help him," she said. "I can't ever see him again."

"But—"

With a sob, she closed the door in my face. I was lucky she'd told me anything at all. Perhaps she'd just needed someone to talk to, but I hadn't the faintest clue how to convince a seer to change her mind.

I left Annabel's house, angling towards home. I'd already texted Nathan apologising for the spectacular catastrophe of yesterday evening but had received no reply yet. I doubted he'd be able to come along for moral support when I went to talk to Steve.

I paused at the fork in the road. I wasn't actually far from his house now. Before I could question whether I was tempting fate, I snapped my fingers, glamouring myself invisible. It wasn't like I'd actually go inside the house. I just wanted to know if he was home.

I flew towards the road of terraced houses. The clamour of raised voices halted me outside Nathan's window, already regretting my rash decision. The window was wide open, and Nathan's father's voice drifted out.

"Absolutely ridiculous, Nathan," Mr Harker thundered. "This place is no fit place for a hunter to live. You know what Jay said—"

"I don't care what he said," Nathan's voice responded. "This is my choice. I have a life here."

"You mean, you have a girlfriend. One of *them.*"

"I liked her," Erin ventured. "She seems a lot of fun."

"Erin, you've always confused 'fun' and 'dangerous'," Mr Harker said.

She snorted. "We hunt magical criminals for a living. They've done a lot worse than rain glitter and sprout wings on us. She's not *dangerous.*"

I felt an unexpected surge of gratitude towards her for defending me, but my heart still sank at Mr Harker's undisguised condemnation. I couldn't deny I'd seen it coming. I'd known Nathan and I would have issues pursuing a relationship from the instant I'd found out I was a fairy, which was why I'd gone to such lengths to keep it from him. My old fears threatened to bubble to the surface. Was there any point in trying to reconcile with people who'd see the worst in me even if I didn't make a public fool of myself? The idea of avoiding Nathan until his family had gone wasn't appealing either—but dragging him into the police's investigation of Terrence's death while his family were in town wasn't an option. I'd have to go it alone.

I flew back to the centre of the town and turned off my invisibility as I neared the jail. Or rather, the place the jail used to be. A new building sat in its place, a huge hulking grey-coloured monstrosity the size of a small manor.

Whoa. This must be the new jail Madame Grey had funded. It looked positively high-tech for something from the magical world. I wasn't sure I liked it, but at least the hunters wouldn't have anything to complain about if they came back to do another inspection. Even a werewolf would have trouble tearing down those walls.

As I stood staring up at the brutal new jail, Steve walked out the front door. "Blair Wilkes," he said. "What are you doing here?"

I snapped on a smile. "Just admiring your new jail. It's very impressive."

He didn't smile back. "Would you like to see the inside?"

"Ah, I think I'll pass." I took a step backwards. "When did you have it built? That was fast."

"Today," he responded. "Those coven witches came and did their fancy trickery. We have cells custom-made for each paranormal, including sirens, elves… and fairies."

I didn't miss the implication in his tone. "Nice work," I said. "Did the prisoners have to be moved out of the place first?" After Blythe's mother's attempted jailbreak, I hoped not.

"The witches did their magic on the old building without moving it," he said, with a disgruntled look over his shoulder. "Not my style, but if it keeps those blasted hunters out…"

Did he even know Nathan's family were here? If not, I wouldn't be enlightening him on the subject.

On the other hand, I'd promised myself I'd at least try. "I don't know if my friend Helen told you, but—I was asked to help her look into Terrence's death."

I braced myself for his usual *well, of course, you involve yourself in every situation involving a dead body, Blair Wilkes* speech. Instead, he gave the jail another scowl. "I wouldn't know. I've been supervising the witches for the last week, so I put Angus in charge of the investigation."

Huh. "So… you haven't arrested any of the students? Helen was pretty worried about that."

"No," he snarled. "I've been here all day making sure the construction work didn't cause any of the prisoners to attempt a quick getaway."

And he marched back into the jail. I stared after him, but he didn't come back out. The way into the police station next door was clear… and Steve wasn't involved in the investigation. Finally, a bit of luck.

I walked into the police station. Unlike the jail, it hadn't undergone a makeover and was still small, cramped, and entirely unsuited for the giant winged person sitting behind the reception desk.

"Did something happen?" I asked Clare, the receptionist. Usually. the gargoyles kept their wings hidden in their slightly-less-alarming human forms.

Clare gave me a scowl. "I just felt like stretching my wings. Steve's had me watching the bloody place all day while those witches did their construction spells."

"At least it's done now," I said. "I'm looking for Angus, if he's around. I'm here on behalf of Helen from the academy." I figured that would get a less hostile response than saying 'the elf king strong-armed me into getting his friends off the hook'. "She's getting concerned about the investigation into her student's death, and I just wanted to clear a couple of things up…"

Clare arched a brow. "Such as? I wasn't aware you were an academy student."

"I take night classes from Helen," I explained. "I heard the elves were accused of the murder. Is that true?"

The gargoyle shifted back into her human form and rose to her feet. "We interviewed two of the students who were at the lake and they said they saw a number of elves in the woods on that day."

"The students said that? Have you spoken to the elves?"

"I'm not in charge of the investigation," Clare said. "And last I checked, neither were you. If the elves wish to defend themselves against the accusation, they'll have to tell us that in person."

I thought so. "They asked me to convince Steve on their behalf," I admitted. "I guess that's not going to go over well, is it? I already know the ones in the woods didn't commit the murder. They didn't lie."

"Is that so?" she said. "I don't need to remind you of Steve's opinion on your… ability, do I? If you're in contact with the elves, ask them to come here and speak for themselves. Nothing else will be acceptable."

Great. Getting Bracken to come here in person would require him to sober up, which seemed impossible. Unless, of course, I found the real culprit. I'd forgotten all about asking the High Fliers if they'd seen anything from the sky. I didn't know where any of them lived, but Helen would be able to tell me.

Which meant one thing: another flying lesson.

7

My second broomstick lesson was as disastrous as the first. While I didn't have a crowd of hyperactive onlookers this time, the broom tossed me off at every opportunity, leaving me bruised and frustrated by the time our allotted hour was up. Even Helen didn't seem to be her usual perky self today, though part of that might be the ongoing lack of updates on Terrence's murder.

There was no good way to broach the subject while falling off a broomstick, so I waited until we were on our way back inside the witches' place before asking, "Have the police come to any more conclusions about Terrence's death yet?"

She shook her head. "No. Not that I've heard, anyway. They haven't come back to the academy since the first questioning."

"Oh," I said. "Apparently, some of them mentioned the elves were seen near the crime scene to the police. So now the elves are mad that they're being accused and want me to straighten it out."

"Why would they want you to do it?" She balanced her broomstick on her shoulder as she opened the door.

"We have… kind of an arrangement. The elf king and me. Long story." I followed her back into the building. "The police won't believe me without proof, so I wondered if you knew who'd accused the elves so we can clear it up." Not that I thought Bracken was innocent by any means, but the other academy students had been the only people aside from the siren who might have an actual motive to kill Terrence. Perhaps the real killer had accused the elves to cover their own tracks.

On the other hand, Bracken hadn't behaved like an innocent person. He'd probably only escaped questioning so far because the gargoyles would never fit into that cave, let alone spot his hiding place. For all I knew, the elves could also use glamour like fairies could. I'd never asked.

"I'm afraid I don't know." Helen led the way to the store cupboard and took my broom from me to put them both neatly away.

"Okay," I said. "Do you know if the police have questioned the High Fliers at all? They were flying over the lake on that day, so one of them might have seen something." I should have asked Clare, but it'd slipped my mind.

She locked the store cupboard. "I'm not on speaking terms with any of the High Fliers. If they're witnesses, I'm sure the police will want to talk to them."

Hmm. It might be worth asking, but the High Fliers weren't my biggest fans, not since I'd rescued Alissa from their clutches when she'd fallen under a personality-altering spell and had to wrestle her off a broomstick in mid-air. Still, if they'd seen anything at all, they might count as witnesses. Then again, they wouldn't be thrilled if I mentioned their names to the police behind their backs. If Helen didn't know them, then I'd need to ask Alissa.

I said goodbye to Helen and made to leave the witches' place, only to spot Rita beckoning me into the classroom. My heart sank to see the disappointment on her face.

"Sorry I'm not making progress." I walked into the classroom. "I don't know why I can't adapt to a broomstick when I can fly just fine on my wings and boots. Maybe that's why the broom won't cooperate with me."

Her lips pursed. "The broomsticks aren't sentient. They're under a spell."

"A spell to make them fly?" I asked.

"Yes. Perhaps there's something interfering with that spell. Do you always wear those boots when you fly?"

"I guess I do," I said. "I can't exactly get rid of the wings, though."

"No, but try without the boots," she said. "You're more than ready to take your Grade Three exams in wand-work and other areas, so there's no reason you shouldn't be able to fly."

My face heated at her words. Rita didn't hand out praise often. "Do witches typically have stronger and weaker areas? Maybe flying is my weak spot."

"Maybe," she said. "However, considering how it's tied to your fairy powers, maybe there's something more going on there."

"I like flying," I said. "I'm just not confident about depending on a stick of wood to keep me up in the air."

"Maybe that's your answer, then. Confidence. Or focus. You were a mile away through most of that lesson. I saw."

"I've had a lot on my mind," I admitted. "Uh, Rita, weird question. Is your divining power like Seeing?"

"It's related," she said. "It's one of the reasons I was assigned as your mentor. Madame Grey suspected your powers were similar to Tanith's, and we didn't have an available tutor with mind-magic. But sensing the truth of a person is similar to sensing the future."

Interesting. "So—my lie-sensing and paranormal-sensing powers are almost a hundred per cent accurate, right? Is it the same for divining?"

"No," she said. "What you can do, Blair, is incredibly rare. Your ability can see through almost any deception. That's not the case for divining powers. Do you remember the divining spells got confused when you first came to town? They couldn't tell if you were a fairy or a witch."

"I don't know about seeing through any deception," I said. "My power got confused a few times." Like when I'd met that pirate ghost by the lake. He'd been a wizard, but after that, he'd been a vampire. If someone was two types of paranormal at once, my ability could only see one of them.

But there was only one time it'd outright refused to work: when I'd encountered Inquisitor Hare, the man who led the hunters and owned the prison where my dad was locked up. When I'd looked at him, I'd been hit by a wave of fear unlike anything I'd ever experienced in my life, and my ability had bounced off an invisible shield. I'd thought the hunters were all humans, but no human had ever set off my paranormal-sensing power before. I suppressed a shiver at the memory.

Rita said, "Every power has its limitations. Even yours. As for divining, I would go as far as to say it's more accurate than Seeing, because you're seeing the present, not the future."

I leapt on that. "Is Seeing always inaccurate? They say old Ava's predictions never come true, but I heard she makes most of them up. I ran into her granddaughter the other day, though, and she seems to take it very seriously."

Rita waved her wand and moved a stack of papers on the desk. "Each seer is different. It's not a common talent. It *is* common for seers to take their powers more seriously as soon as a prediction comes true. However, if one vision turns out to be real, it doesn't necessarily mean everything will."

"How does it work?" I asked. "Is it like dreams or visions, or is it like my power, where they look at a person and just… know things?"

"It's different for each seer," Rita said. "Ava… as far as I remember, she used a crystal ball. That helps focus her powers."

"What's Annabel's, do you know?"

"Why the sudden interest?"

"She claimed she recently developed the gift but had no signs before," I explained. "She also ended her relationship with her boyfriend because she had a vision of them breaking up, but she said he wouldn't have had reason to end it otherwise, and… I don't know, it seemed weird. Is that normal for seers?"

"I'm no expert on the seeing gift, but it behaves in ways unlike other types of innate magic. Perhaps it's possible to develop the gift in adulthood… but Madame Grey is the person to ask, not me."

"I thought she said Seeing was wishy-washy," I said. "Anyway, Annabel broke up with her boyfriend—an elf—and he went off the rails. Now he's a potential witness to Terrence's death, except he was so drunk that day he doesn't remember any of it. I wondered if I could get Annabel to talk to him…"

"Blair," said Rita admonishingly. "I thought you might have taken a break from encroaching on Steve's territory."

"Helen asked me to help out," I said, but I knew it wasn't worth pushing the issue. "I thought Steve was too occupied with the new jail. I didn't know Madame Grey was going to put it together that fast."

"Oh, you've seen it?" she asked. "It took an entire coven to construct the place without removing any of the prisoners, but with hunters in town, it was better to act sooner rather than later."

"Hunters?" I echoed. "If you mean Nathan's family, they're not on duty."

"Blair, I'm sure you know well that everything they witness in the town will make it back to the main branch. We're taking no chances."

"Oh." That meant the Inquisitor would hear all about the glitter, my cat, the elves and the pixie. Maybe then he'd strike me off his list of people to hire. There had to be a silver lining somewhere. "All right, I just wondered. See you in a bit."

I didn't need a seeing ability or lack thereof to sense that the universe had no intention of giving me a break. And I still hadn't heard from Nathan.

———

When I reached home, it was to find Alissa buried under a pile of cats. Or rather, cat. Whenever Roald tried to snuggle close to Alissa, Sky batted him away.

"He's being downright needy today," she said, her voice muffled by Sky's fur.

"Again? Sky, what is it?" I walked to the sofa and he practically threw himself at me, purring like a lawnmower. "What's with him?"

She sat upright and lifted Roald into her lap. "You tell me that. I've been at the hospital all day chasing patients around who escaped from the ward for long term residents."

"What, Old Ava?"

She shuddered. "Don't talk to me about that woman. She's going through a phase of trying to wander out of the ward whenever anyone looks away from her. I think she needs a friend, but there's only her granddaughter to take care of her and… never mind. How'd the lesson go?"

I sat down on the sofa, and Sky sprawled on my lap. "Alissa, do you know how to get hold of the leader of the High Fliers?"

Her brows shot up. "The lesson went that well?"

"No, it was a disaster. Again." I stroked Sky behind the ears. "But the High Fliers might have seen what happened to Terrence. They can see everything from up in the air. It's the last lead I have now."

"Ah," she said. "I guess you didn't manage to get through to Steve? You didn't try, did you?"

"His friend Angus is the one in charge of this investigation," I said. "But Clare—the receptionist—seemed convinced he wouldn't budge unless I get the elf to go there in person. Which is about as likely as Steve joining the High Fliers himself."

"The leader of the High Fliers is named Robyn," Alissa said. "She'll be running another practise session by the lake tomorrow. Not sure she'll speak to you after last time, though."

"I'll deal with it," I said. "The elves want me to do the impossible. Bracken is totally addled, and I think the only way to get him to sober up is to get Annabel to talk some sense into him. But she's certain she did the right thing in ending their relationship."

"You spoke to her, right?" She stroked Roald, who purred.

"Yeah, she's absolutely convinced she has the seeing gift and it was the right thing to do. Did Ava mention her?"

"No, she didn't," Alissa said. "I mean, she predicted all our doom a dozen times, but that's standard. And tried to curse us. We locked her wand up in storage ages ago, but half the staff are outright refusing to work on her ward now."

"Ouch." I winced. "Yeah, sounds rough. So she's still giving out bogus predictions?"

"Yep. Like I said, standard. I wouldn't think Annabel would take her own visions seriously after hearing Ava's rants."

"Rita told me seeing is way less accurate than divining," I said. "Or anything else. I wonder what prompted her to take that vision seriously? There must be another reason."

"Miaow." Sky prodded my pocket. My phone buzzed. Nathan. Oh, no. I was not ready for this conversation. I might never be ready.

Alissa raised a questioning eyebrow. I mouthed *Nathan* at her. She mimed answering the phone.

No time like the present. I took my phone into the bedroom so the cats wouldn't interrupt and tapped the screen.

"Hi," I said. "Uh. Sorry about the other day."

"There's no need to apologise, Blair," he said. "I got your messages. Besides, I think you gave Erin more entertainment than she's had in months."

"I thought hunters' lives were always entertaining." Oops. Maybe I shouldn't have brought it up. But I'd gone to such lengths to avoid mentioning the subject during that disastrous evening and it'd all fallen to pieces anyway.

"I told the elves that they're not to interrupt me again," I said, when he didn't respond for a moment. "The reason they did that in the first place was because I brushed them off when they tried to ambush me on the way to work. And as for the pixie, I don't know why he flipped out like that. I thought Sky understood that he's not supposed to follow me to important events, so I don't know why he felt the need to show up."

"Maybe it was too soon," Nathan said. "To meet my entire family at once, I mean."

My heart sank. "Okay. I understand that."

Please don't let this be going where I think it is.

"Erin is insistent on seeing you again before she leaves town," he said. "I wondered if you wanted to come on a walk with us this weekend."

"Really?" What, he wasn't breaking up with me? Or keeping me at arm's reach until his family left and I could get away with unleashing havoc to my heart's content? "I should be able to manage that. Are they staying all weekend, then?"

"They're heading back up north on Sunday," he replied. "That okay? It's fine if you want to sit this one out."

I should, for all our sakes, but I hadn't seen him all week. My resolve weakened. I couldn't do anything too heinous on a walk, right?

"It's been a long week, but I want to see you." He'd given me a second chance, but considering my track record, it was risky. Especially with Terrence's death and the elf king's demand hanging over my head.

"I miss you, too, Blair," he said. "See you soon, okay?"

I clicked off my phone, more determined than ever to resolve the case. For a start, I needed to question the High Fliers.

———

I made my way to the lake after work the following day. Despite Rob's constant presence, the workday had been relatively low-stress. Maybe there was something to be said for having a highly efficient werewolf in the office who dealt with all the problem clients. Better than nothing, and definitely better than Blythe.

As I'd expected, the High Fliers were swooping around the lake in their usual death-defying formations when I went down the path to the shore. I stood and watched for a minute, then I walked to the lake's edge. A number of merpeople swam in the shallows, waving at me. I recognised one of them as the blue-haired merman who'd found Terrence's body.

"Hey," I said, waving back. "Is that elf here, do you know?"

The merpeople turned away to converse among themselves. After a moment, the merman who'd found Terrence's body swam away from the group to join me.

"Hello, Blair," he said. "The others are worried about the police coming back."

"Is that likely?" I indicated the sloping hill leading to the falls. "You did see the elf, right? He's a suspect... did you know?"

"Him? No." His eyes widened. "No, he didn't kill the boy. I was helping him hide his bottles when the body washed into the river."

Truth. "Wait, so he didn't drown under the falls, then?"

That meant he must have drowned in the lake and either washed into the river... or someone had moved his body into the cave.

"Not when I was there." He lowered his gaze, shame on his face. "The elf's people were shouting at him, saying he was a disgrace. I felt sorry for him."

"Thanks for telling me," I said. "I'm going to talk to the High Fliers and see if they spotted anything from the sky."

I walked away from the shore, more certain than ever that Terrence hadn't drowned by the falls. If the merman told the truth—and my lie-sensing power told me he did—it meant that the High Fliers were more likely to have spotted him. They couldn't see the falls, but the rest of the lake was visible from up in the air.

When the broomsticks landed on the ground in a swoop of bright-coloured cloaks, I waited for the other High Fliers to leave, hovering at the edge of the woods to avoid being spotted. It was a wonder they could fly at all in those costumes, but I supposed those huge cloaks would act as effective parachutes if they fell off their brooms.

Seeing the witch who led the High Fliers was alone, I approached her. Robyn wore a bright purple hat which must be magicked to stay attached to her head, since it never fell off even when she was hanging upside-down in mid-air.

"Oh, it's you," she said, in less than enthusiastic tones. "I'm afraid it's too late to join our summer event, but there's a waiting list for the next one."

"Er, I'm still at a beginner's broomstick level," I said quickly. "But I wondered if I could ask you a question? It's about the student… the one who drowned over the weekend. You were here, right?"

"Yes, we were," she said. "Terribly sad. Accidental drowning, was it?"

"Not sure about an accident," I said. "The police are investigating it as a potential murder, and I wondered if any of your people might have seen anything. You know, from up in the air. He drowned in the lake, but his body was found near the falls."

"Not to my knowledge," she said. "Are you helping the police with the investigation, then?"

"I'm helping Helen. She's my tutor for broomstick lessons and she was in charge of the students on that day, so I thought I'd ask. Since there aren't any reliable witnesses from ground level, I wondered if any of your fliers had seen anything."

"Well, I can certainly ask," she said. "I like Helen. She has spirit."

I wasn't sure if she was implicitly saying I *didn't*, but I'd expected her to refuse to help me after I'd yanked Alissa out of their ranks. But Robyn seemed pretty level-headed for someone who spent most of her free time hanging upside-down from a broomstick.

"Thanks," I said gratefully. "That'd really help."

Robyn leapt on her broom and zipped over the lake to some of the departing fliers, stopping them in their tracks. I followed more slowly around the shore, wishing there was a spell I could use to borrow some of her broomstick-riding talent for the exam. It seemed ridiculous that every single member of the group had more talent than fifty of me put together. Maybe I could body-swap with a High Flier for the duration of the broomstick test. Or at least ask them for useful tips. I'd bet none of them had ever tutored a fairy witch before.

By the time I caught up to their group, several of the fliers waited, looking at me curiously. All of them wore bright cloaks and carried their broomsticks on their shoulders.

A pale woman wearing red was the first to speak. "You're Blair, right? Robyn said you wanted to talk to us."

"I just wondered if any of you saw what went on at the lake on Sunday," I said. "When Terrence drowned. Did you see anyone fall in?"

"I did," she said. "A boy and a girl. They climbed out afterwards, though. It looked like they were having fun."

"Oh, I think I saw that," I said, recalling when I'd spotted two people fall off a broom into the lake. "But I wasn't really paying attention."

"They tried to mimic our broomstick-hopping," said a dark-skinned witch wearing blue. "This boy tried to jump onto the back of the girl's broom. I think he was trying to impress someone."

Trying to impress someone… like the sirens? "Did you see what he looked like?"

"No, we were too high up," said the blue-cloaked witch.

Maybe it'd been Terrence, maybe not, but he hadn't

drowned until later in the evening. "Did you see anyone near the woods, or on the path to the falls?"

"There was another student," she said. "I heard them yelling at him, and they called him Claude, I think. He kept dive-bombing people and knocking them off their brooms."

Hmm. Claude wasn't someone I'd questioned. I'd need to go back to the academy if I wanted to find out if he'd been involved.

"Okay," I said to them. "Thanks."

I turned away, my phone buzzing with a message. I expected it to be Nathan, but found a disgruntled text from Alissa saying she'd had her shift extended thanks to a certain old mischief-making seer.

Looked like I was back to square one—unless I talked sense into the elf or jogged his memory. If only Annabel could do that, then it was worth speaking to Ava about her granddaughter's sudden ability to see the future. If nothing else, talking to the old seer might give poor Alissa a break.

8

<hr>

Ava wasn't hard to find. She spotted me the instant I walked into the hospital waiting room and crowed with delight. As usual, she wore a purple wig with a plastic wand tangled in it and a dress patterned with bright flowers.

"Let's go on an adventure, young Briar," she said, grabbing my arm.

"Uh, great idea, but you're not supposed to be out of the ward," I said. "Also, it's Blair."

Ava seemed confused about me at the best of times. She might have known my mother and had been the one to tell me my maternal grandmother had died shortly after her daughter had left town, but she never managed to get my name right.

"Beware the wild one, Briar Wilkes," she said. "Beware the wild one."

Okay... "Who's the wild one?" I decided to humour her. "You mean the elves?"

She spun on the spot in a dramatic dance. "Elves? Tricksters, they are. Nasty little tricksters."

"Have you seen any elves in your visions lately?" I asked, in a desperate attempt to get her to sit down.

"I see water," she said. "I see glass. I see death."

Right. I knew better than to wonder if she was having an actual premonition. "Have you seen Annabel this week?"

"Oh, not for a while," she said. "She hasn't got the time for the likes of me, not now she's spending all her time with that elf. Never mind her, let's go on an adventure."

"Hang on." I moved my arms behind my back in case she grabbed me again. "Did you know they split up? Understandably, Annabel's not happy. I wondered if she'd talked to you about it."

"Split up?" She sat down next to me. "No, no. She never said anything to me."

I hesitated. "Well, she split up with him and they're both very upset. The thing is… did she ever talk to you about developing the Seeing gift?"

"No." Her glassy blue-grey eyes clouded over in a manner similar to her granddaughter's. "No, she didn't develop the gift when she hoped she would. We were both disappointed, but these things are rare. What you and I have is a *gift*, Briar."

"What if she did develop it, though?" I asked. "What then?"

"I would need to teach her," she said. "No seer can learn without guidance."

Hmm. Either Annabel had found a mentor, or she'd gone it alone. But she had so much faith in her vision that something must have convinced her that it was real.

"Of course, if she had the gift, she'd tell me," Ava said. "She tells me everything. Even about that elf."

Maybe not everything. That was a conversation those two needed to have in their own time.

If most of what Ava said was nonsense or unreliable at best, maybe that was why Annabel had opted not to tell her.

Still, most of the time, witches and wizards discovered their gifts in childhood. I was one of the few exceptions. If she hadn't asked her grandmother for advice, who had taught her? I'd thought there weren't any other seers in town. Unless she'd self-taught, but her level of conviction in her own vision suggested there was something more going on.

"If you see something in a vision, does it always come true?" I asked. "I mean, how did you go about predicting the future?"

She dropped her voice to a whisper. "I used a crystal ball," she said. "People say it doesn't work, but it does. When you gaze into the depths of the crystal, you *see*. Doesn't mean what you see is necessarily *useful*. You might see that your friend is going to get a cold, or it's going to rain at the summer picnic. Of course, it's often already happened by the time the vision's taken place."

"Oh," I said. "If, say, you saw yourself breaking up with a partner in a vision, and it hadn't already happened yet, would it then come true no matter what?"

"The future isn't set in stone," she said. "Because people can't be predicted. We can see natural disasters, and other such occurrences, but in terms of people's decisions... it gets murky."

Huh. That actually made a kind of sense. Unless I was starting to lose my wits, too.

"Maybe you can talk to Annabel about it?" I suggested. "She seems convinced, and I'm not a seer so I can't offer her advice. Perhaps you could ask the nurses to get in touch with her for you?"

"Tanith had an uncanny gift for reading people, too," she said. "But not all. Beware the wild one... beware him."

"Beware who?" I looked into her glassy eyes. "Ava, who are you talking about? Do you mean the elves?"

"Ava, why are you out of your room?" Lou, a petite Asian

nurse whose uniform was covered in what looked like green slime, came into the waiting room. "Blair, what're you doing here?"

"I was waiting for Alissa." Over Ava's shoulder, I mouthed, *I was trying to stop her from getting outside.* Technically true, but part of me wished I could finish our conversation. *Who in the world is the wild one?*

Lou sighed. "Ava, you know the rules. I'm guessing Alissa got diverted by that pesky goblin again."

"I won't be taken alive!" Ava proclaimed, bouncing to her feet again and making for the doors.

"Ah." I moved to block her way, wondering if she'd flip out if I drew my wand.

"A hex on you." Ava yanked her own wand from her hair and waved it at me. Lucky for all of us that the staff had replaced her real wand with a fake one the instant she'd got it back. "A hex on you all!"

"Ava, come with me and we'll talk," I said. "You don't want to go out there. It's going to rain."

Probably true, considering the upcoming broomstick contest. To my astonishment—and Lou's, come to that—Ava followed my lead when I beckoned her down the corridor to the ward for long-term patients.

"Lou, has she seen her granddaughter recently?" I asked.

The nurse blinked. "Annabel calls every week. Ava talked to her for hours on the phone last weekend."

"Oh," I said. "She said she hadn't seen Annabel in a while, so I assumed that meant she hadn't called."

Annabel must have avoided mentioning her breakup—not to mention her newfound talent. Weird. If anything, her grandmother might have been the one person who could offer helpful advice in that particular area. Even if her visions were inaccurate, she was bound to have a few tips for a beginner.

"I think Ava does most of the talking," Lou added, pushing open the ward doors to let us through.

"Makes sense." I walked into the ward and beckoned Ava to follow me. "Annabel's going through a hard time at the moment. Maybe Ava can help."

"A hex on all of you!" Ava yelled at everyone in the ward.

Or maybe not.

———

As the next day was Saturday, there were no classes at the academy. Helen had mentioned taking some of the students to the lake to prepare for the big Sky Hopper match, though. I'd rather swim with the fishes than go anywhere near another broomstick, but it would be the only chance I'd have to question the students without waiting until Monday.

My mind, however, was full of Ava, Annabel and crystal balls. I considered paying Annabel another visit, but I doubted she'd seen Terence's drowning in the crystal ball.

Alissa went with me to the lake for moral support, so we could claim to be practising magic if Helen tried to rope me into volunteering as a referee.

"It's not a pleasant day for it," Alissa commented, indicating the cloudy sky. "Oh—the High Fliers are over there, too."

"Of course they are." I watched the bright colours of their cloaks swooping over the lake. "Better hope the clouds don't stick around, because that looks downright dangerous to do in the rain." Their broomsticks yo-yoed around as though trying to win prizes for how many times they could shake their riders without anyone falling off. The fliers must use a spell to keep their balance, because there'd be a lot more accidents otherwise.

Helen stood on the bank among a small group of

students, watching the fliers. Her hair was dishevelled and there were shadows under her eyes, but she gave me a smile.

"Blair," she said, back to her usual bright self in front of the students. "There are a couple of students who'd like to talk to you."

She indicated a tall guy who very much did *not* look like he wanted to talk to me. He was huge, hulking, and had 'school bully' written all over him.

"Hey," I said. "I'm Blair."

"I know," he said, scowling. "I saw you questioning the others. Helen thinks I was pushing people into the water. Someone couldn't keep their mouth shut." He shot a glare at the other students.

"Well, were you?" He must be Claude, the boy the High Fliers had seen fooling around by the lake.

"Yes. I didn't kill Terrence, though. I was only messing about."

Truth. I looked at the rest of the group. "Did anyone see two people fall into the water?" I asked. "I heard someone tried to jump onto another person's broom, like the High Fliers."

"That was Terrence," a blond girl put in. "He thought it was funny to jump onto Sherry's broom, and they both fell in."

"Oh," I said. "How long before he drowned was this?"

"Dunno, I wasn't keeping time," said the girl. "We were all drunk. He thought it would impress her."

"Impress… who?" I scanned the group.

She pointed to a girl with braided hair and dark skin who I recognised as the student who'd said she was a healer. "Sherry."

"It was a stupid joke," Sherry said, her voice shaky. "He was too drunk to fly and could barely swim at that point, even with his magic. But I made sure he got out and he was fine. He called me a spoilsport and took off. I didn't think he'd run off to the falls and—and—"

"But you think it was an accident?"

"Why wouldn't it be?" she said. "He was drunk and acting idiotic. He hardly knew his own name, let alone his magical power. The last time I saw him alive was when he ran off after we got out of the water."

Truth. "Okay. Thanks for telling me."

I walked back to Helen. "Neither of them did it," I said in an undertone. "Do you know if it's possible for a witch or wizard to forget how to use their power? I mean, when drunk?"

"It depends on the power," she said, her mouth pinched. "I mean, theoretically, anyone can forget how to use their power if it isn't an intuitive one. If he was that drunk, I'd normally be worried about him *overusing* his power—getting into fights, things like that. But everyone is different."

"Well, mine is more of a background noise," I said. "I barely notice it most of the time, and there's been a couple of times when it's switched off…"

Only twice, in fact. Once was when a vampire employee at the university had used his own power to put mine on mute.

The other was when I'd encountered the siren's song for the first time.

Could a siren's song make a person forget how to use magic? Maybe. If so, the siren might not even have had to be near to him at the time to cause him to forget how to use his water-controlling power to save his own life.

Of all the suspects, the siren I'd spoken to was most likely to have the *ability* to counter Terrence's power, but I didn't want to jump to any conclusions without proof.

"Any luck?" Alissa asked when I returned to her side, leaving the students to resume their game.

"No." I shook my head, frustrated. "The other students all said they didn't do it and my lie-sensing power didn't pick up on anything weird. The thing is… do you remember when that siren's ability caused my lie-sensing power to turn off? Might it have the same effect on other magical powers?"

Her eyes widened. "Yes. It's possible. The sirens' song confuses the senses. I mean, I can use my healing power when I'm drunk, but I've never tried to use it while listening to a siren's song."

"Maybe it would dampen your powers," I said. "It's powerful. I don't know, though. The sirens would need to be close by for it to work."

"So the elf might be innocent?"

"I have no idea. Maybe *he* heard the siren's song—"

Shouting drew our attention to the lake. A cluster of brooms had descended in a cloud of bright cloaks to land on the shore, where a body lay face down in the shallows, a long blue cloak billowing on the surface.

"Oh, no," said Alissa. "One of the High Fliers fell in again."

She moved closer to the group, pulling out her wand. "Hey!" she said. "I'm a healer! Let me through."

The High Fliers moved back, depositing the limp body on the bank. Alissa wove through the crowd, but looked at me a moment later, her expression grim. She didn't need to say it. The High Flier was dead.

9

Everyone stood and stared at the body as though hoping that Alissa would be able to perform a miracle, but even a magically gifted healer couldn't bring back the dead. That long cloak had one major drawback—it was a dead weight when waterlogged and was impossible to swim in.

Alissa lifted her head to face the others. "I'm sorry."

A murmur passed through the High Fliers.

"That's unfair," one of them said. "You're a healer. Why can't you bring her back? She couldn't have been in the water long."

"That's why we warn you about practising so close to the lake," Alissa said, a tremor in her voice. "I'm so sorry, but there's nothing more I can do."

The rest of the High Fliers landed beside the bank, crowding around to look at her. Alissa and I backed away from the lake, and I spotted Helen gathering the students at a distance to stop them from getting too close.

Alissa's mouth pinched. "It was bound to happen eventually. There have been a few close calls this summer already."

"But you're sure it was an accident?" I dropped my voice, but a couple of the High Fliers glanced in our direction.

"Laurie was one of our best fliers," said a young Indian woman wearing a bright red cloak and pointed hat. "She wasn't trying anything complicated, was she?"

"I didn't see," put in an older woman with a pink-and-white hat perched on top of her grey bob. "But she's been flying since she was old enough to hold a broom."

Even an experienced flier could fall victim to a siren. I stood on tiptoe to see over the group but didn't spot any sirens close by. The merpeople had spotted the ruckus and swam to the shallows. I walked past the gathering crowd until I found a clear spot to view the lake. Its surface rippled with gold, reflecting the sun—and a brighter flash of light caught my eye from the west side of the lake. Then another flash, like a lightning bolt.

"What's that flashing?" Alissa caught up to me, breathless. "Is that coming from the falls?"

"Good question." I peered to my left, but it was impossible to tell from this angle. It looked like lightning. Or magic. "I'm going to find out who it is."

Someone called Alissa's name. As she moved over to help, I tapped on my Seven Millimetre Boots and flew uphill in search of the source of the flashing lights.

I already suspected who might be the cause. Sure enough, Bracken stood so close to the edge of the path up alongside the lake, it was a small miracle he hadn't fallen in himself. His hands were outstretched, and bolts of light shot into the air like miniature fireworks.

"Hey, stop that!" I told him. "Did you just knock a witch off a broomstick?"

He whirled on me, and a bolt of lightning shot past my head. I jumped, nearly tripping over the edge myself.

"Watch out," he slurred.

"What are you doing?" I asked.

He hiccoughed. "Nothing, nothing. She used to like it when I summoned the lights, but now I have an audience of one."

"Did you see someone fall into the water just then?" I asked. "Did your lightning hit someone?" Surely someone would have seen if it had, right?

"There's nobody in the water," he slurred.

"There isn't now," I said. "Come on, get away from the edge before you fall in."

Honestly. Even if he'd knocked her from her broom by accident, an innocent woman was still dead. The police would have a hard time getting a confession out of him if he didn't remember anything, but the situation didn't look good.

"Why are you here?" He meandered down the path with surprising agility from someone who could barely speak.

"I'm here because someone just died." I tapped on my boots again and followed him. "Are you sure you don't remember?" Now I looked out across the lake, it seemed unlikely that he'd managed to hit her broom from this far off —but how else had she fallen in? "Can you remember any more about last weekend?"

"I remember nothing after she left me." He hiccoughed, swaying to the left, then the right.

"Annabel," I said. "Did she ever mention having the sight before? Because a few months ago, she couldn't see the future at all."

He tripped downhill a few steps. "She saw herself breaking off the relationship, that's enough for me."

"But when did it start?" I prodded, resisting the impulse to turn him in and see if Steve's interrogation chamber did a better job of prompting his memory.

"She ended it, not started it." He slumped, sitting down on a rock. "Nothing I do will ever let me forget her."

"So you do remember?" I asked. "She must have mentioned her grandmother to you, right? Ava is a seer, but Annabel didn't have the gift until recently."

"Seeing? Yes… she saw… she had a crystal ball."

Now we were getting somewhere. "Did she mention having a mentor?" I asked. "Because her grandmother said that she couldn't learn without someone to teach her."

"Ava," he said. "No, no, she told me not to tell Ava."

"About what?"

There came a loud screeching from the shore, and he jumped violently, tipping onto his side. "Abomination!"

"That's the gargoyles," I said. "I told you, someone just drowned. Are you positive your magical lightning didn't hit someone on a broom?"

If I turned him in, I could say goodbye to ever getting any help from the elves. If I didn't, an innocent woman's death might go unpunished. Not to mention I'd be in trouble myself if Steve found out I'd been talking to Bracken. But the only way to jog his memory was for him to sober up, which would take too long. There *were* memory potions, but I didn't know if they worked on alcohol-induced memory loss.

The elf snapped his fingers and vanished. I blinked at the spot where he'd stood, stupefied. That answered the question about whether or not elves could use glamour, then.

Shuffling footsteps retreated downhill, telling me he was getting away. I hovered on the spot, mentally kicking myself. I could just picture Steve's face if I reported an invisible elf as responsible for a crime. From the sound of Bracken's stumbling, there was a risk of him falling into the water, too, but since I couldn't see him, he'd have to swim to shore alone if he did.

Three more gargoyles landed on the shore. I turned my

back, leaving the elf behind. Nothing for it—I'd have to come and speak to him again when he'd de-glamoured and turned visible again.

As luck would have it, Steve spotted me as I approached the High Fliers again.

"Blair Wilkes," he said. "How did I guess you were involved?"

"Blair was with me," Alissa said. "Laurie was flying over the lake when she fell off her broom."

Steve grunted. "Practising magic, were you? I've heard stories about the chaos you cause whenever you have a wand in your hand."

"It'd take more than that to bring down a High Flier's broomstick," Alissa said, narrowing her eyes at him. "Blair didn't even have her wand out."

Steve grunted and turned to speak to the High Fliers' leader. I hovered on the spot, undecided. If the elf reappeared later, I'd come back for a second questioning and hope he was more willing to talk this time. Until then, I doubted Steve would appreciate being led on a wild elf chase.

Beware the wild one, old Ava had said. No kidding.

I saw the red-cloaked High Flier a few metres away, dabbing at her eyes.

"Hey," I said to her. "Steve finished interrogating you?"

"For now." Her eyes shone with tears. "This makes no sense. She had the skill to fly through a storm and come out in one piece."

"I'm sorry for your loss," I said, my gut twisting. Mentioning the elf would only make things worse, but I wished I knew how to help.

"I don't think it was an accident," she said quietly. "But why would anyone kill her? We're all on the same team."

"Did you see anything before she fell?" I asked. "I mean, maybe something hit her broom and knocked her in."

"I doubt it," she said hoarsely. "Our brooms are fitted with spells which prevent us from slipping and to protect us against misfiring spells from our own wands, extreme weather conditions, things like that."

"Wait, they're protected from every type of magic?" Even an elf's magical lightning? I'd bet that also fell into the category of 'extreme weather conditions'.

"I don't know about every type, but unless someone flew into her in mid-air and physically pushed her off, it can't have happened via magic."

That changes things. Unless it was a siren's song that'd caused her to fall, but no sign of them appeared in the lake. Just quiet, still water, a growing crowd—and no elves in sight.

———

Sky woke me up on Sunday by prodding me in the leg with his claw. I sat bolt upright, wincing. I hadn't slept well, and I'd almost forgotten I was supposed to be meeting Nathan's family again.

I'd spent yesterday evening looking up possible ways to jog the elf's memory without causing him to glamour himself invisible or throw me in the lake. Alissa had suggested replacing the alcohol in his bottles with a potion designed to clear his mind. If I wanted to go the clandestine route, there were substitution spells that would let me transplant my own concoction into the elf's bottle without him knowing, but that would require finding him—a tricky task if he was still invisible.

Sky gave me another vigorous poke with his claw.

"Ow. Okay, I'm getting up." I climbed out of bed, glancing out the window. "Normal," I whispered. "Sky, I'm going to be completely normal today."

"Miaow."

"Who am I kidding? Myself for one." I ran around my room in search of clean clothes. *Great start... I'm having a one-sided conversation with my cat.*

In the end, I selected a plain T-shirt and jeans. Wearing anything nice on a hike was a waste of time. I also decided to wear my Seven Millimetre Boots. They were the most suitable boots I had for hiking, and after the glitter incident, I doubted anyone would bat an eyelid if I started levitating.

A text came from Nathan—*Meet us by the lake.*

Wait. I'd hoped they wanted to walk in the nearby hills, not by the lake. Nathan must know about the High Flier's death by this point, but I'd bet he'd neglected to mention it to his family. The High Fliers shouldn't be around, but I hoped the merpeople and sirens avoided the shore, for all our sakes.

After I'd dressed and showered, I told Sky firmly to stay put, bribing him with a bowl of his favourite food. Then I left the flat, hoping I hadn't made a mistake by not handing the elf over to the authorities. I doubted they could keep their hands on a drunk, invisible elf who really didn't want to be caught, but he *and* the sirens had better stay as far from the shore as possible if they didn't want a run-in with Nathan's family.

I used my levitating boots to save time until I reached the road leading to the lake, then landed and walked the normal way to the shore. Emphasis on 'normal'.

Nathan and the others were already there, waiting for me. *Here we go.*

"Hi," I said, wishing I'd spent the night looking up a spell to erase *their* memories of the other evening instead. "It's a lovely day."

Spectacular conversationalist, I was not. Nor was I a great tour guide, especially when they wouldn't want to hear about anything magical. *Here's the cave where the drunken elf lives, and here's the pirate ship which used to be haunted by a wizard's ghost.* Yeah, not happening.

"I suppose it's picturesque, at least," Mr Harker commented.

"Yes, it is. Especially in summer," I said. Normal. I could do normal. "I think we should walk… this way." I vaguely gestured in the opposite direction from the woods.

"Where are the falls?" asked Erin.

So much for that idea. "They're up the path by the woods, but you don't want to go there."

"Why not?" she asked.

Everyone looked at me, Nathan included.

I shrugged. "We'd have to walk by the forest. The path's slippery and not that safe."

Stop talking, Blair. I was with a group of people who'd all hunted rogue werewolves for a living. A slippery path wouldn't bother them a bit. They were also dressed more appropriately for hiking than I was.

"Right, the paranormals divide up their forest into territories, don't they?" Nathan's father said. "They seem to do that everywhere."

Jay nodded. "Yes. Most of our calls are because one of those shifters has accused another of trespassing on their territory. You'd think they'd do a better job of marking it out to avoid these situations."

"It'd be simpler if they didn't live near human towns at all," Mr Harker said.

I fidgeted, hoping there weren't any shifters nearby. The last thing I needed was to have to mediate a fight between a hunter and a werewolf.

"Absolutely," Jay said. "Separate territories are what they need, as far from one another as possible."

"I assume you'd ask the shifters first without making

assumptions about what they need?" The words came out before I could stop them.

Mr Harker scowled at me. I looked past him—and froze. A small figure staggered beside the lake, a bottle dangling from his hand... and very much visible. *Oh no.*

"Let's go this way!" I stepped to the right, away from the lake. "There are hills... and fields." *Note to self: never go into tourism.*

"There's an elf," Erin said, staring at Bracken. "And... is that a wine bottle?"

I sent a silent plea to Bracken not to notice us, but worse, Erin moved in his direction. I hurried behind her, though I hadn't the faintest clue what to do. It was too late to stop the others from seeing him. I winced at their shocked murmurs as the elf staggered to the side, the bottle dragging on the muddy shore.

"I remember the crystal ball, Blair Wilkes," he proclaimed, before vomiting on his own shoes and passing out.

"Friend of yours?" Erin asked me.

"Nope," I said. "Definitely not."

"He knew your name," Jay said.

"Everyone knows my name," I said stupidly.

"Right, you're notorious." Erin winked.

I wished I could evaporate on the spot. "No, I'm just the newest citizen in town."

"I thought the elves didn't live in the town," Eric observed, eying the elf's unconscious body.

"Uh, they live in the forest." Of all the times for the High Fliers not to be here to distract everyone.

"We should take him home, since the forest is right there," Erin said. "He's adorable, isn't he?"

"He's drunk," commented Mr Harker. "And off his territory."

"This is more neutral territory," Nathan said. "Anyone can come to the lake via the main paths."

"I know where he lives," I said. "I can take him home." If he woke up and heard one of them make a disparaging comment about the elves, he might start shooting lightning bolts, which was the last thing any of us needed.

I pulled out my wand. Erin mimed ducking for cover and Eric laughed. I flushed, but gave my wand a flick, levitating the unconscious elf into the air. Jay and Eric stepped back out of range as though expecting me to drop the elf on them. As for Mr Harker, he must think I was completely deranged by now.

I am never going to live this down. If Nathan and I get married, Erin is going to tell this story at every single family gathering for the rest of my life. Along with the pixie incident.

A merman popped up out of the water, watching me levitate the elf uphill. "What are you doing?" he asked.

"Helping him back to his hideout," I said. "He mentioned a crystal ball. Does he do that often?"

"Crystal ball?" He shook his head. "No, he's never mentioned it before."

"Never mind."

I left the elf on the slope leading down to the falls, wishing I'd brewed up a memory potion after all. Or a spell that would turn me into a tree for a few years until the humiliation of the last week wore off.

———

"Blair, let me do this bit," said Alissa.

Trusting her expertise, I let her take over the potion making. We'd opted for a cross between one of the anti-hangover potions the local pub put in the witch cocktails and a potion that enhanced clarity of the mind, using Alissa's advanced textbook. We took it in turns to cut up the leaves and scatter powders and herbs into the small cauldron I'd got as part of my basic potion-making kit. The potion was not for beginners, but Alissa said she'd used a similar version to help out the notorious elf who kept ending up in hospital due to his drunken exploits.

Sky wound around my ankles, purring. "Hey," I said, scratching behind his ears. "I don't suppose you've seen the pixie?"

"What do you need him for?" Alissa asked.

I crouched down to give Sky a proper stroke. "No reason. I just haven't seen him for a while. Unless he thinks I'm going to yell at him for screwing things up with Nathan."

"I thought it was the elf this time."

"Don't even remind me." I shuddered. "Erin found the whole thing hilarious, but the others looked like they wanted to have me committed. And I wasn't the one who collapsed drunkenly into a lake."

"Maybe you should have stayed at home."

"I realise that now." I ripped up a few leaves and tossed them into the cauldron. "I only helped the elf because Nathan's father and brother were saying some questionable things about the elf community and I didn't want him to wake up and throw a bolt of lightning at them."

"Ouch." She looked into the cauldron. "To be honest, that elf sounds like a lost cause. Are you sure this potion will work?"

"I'm the one who's supposed to be asking that question." I sighed. "I have to try. Wouldn't hurt to find out why Annabel can suddenly see the future either. I feel like it's connected."

"You only need to prove his innocence, right?" Alissa delicately chopped up a few stems with a sharp knife.

"Yeah, but I'm not sure he is. He was shooting magical lightning over the lake when the High Flier fell off her broom. They say the brooms are protected, but who knows how elf magic works?"

"He was shooting it from his hands?" she asked. "Huh. I didn't know elves could do that."

"Nor me, until he did it." I threw more leaves into the cauldron, my temper sizzling like the flames on the stove. I was mostly annoyed at myself. Nathan's family thought I was a freak. The pixie had ditched me, the elves were indifferent to the fact that one of them might be a murderer, and no other suspects had shown up in relation to the High Flier's death.

I was sure the two deaths were linked, but until Bracken got his senses back, guesswork was all we'd have. I needed to be as devious as an elf to get a confession from him.

10

Dawn came, and I forced myself awake so I could take the potion to the lake before work. Since Alissa had supervised every step, I was confident the potion wouldn't poison him. Now all I needed was to *find* the elf, assuming he wasn't still invisible.

"Better hope it works." I lined up a row of empty bottles on the kitchen table to practise the swapping spell again. As I waved my wand, the potion leapt from one bottle to the next without spilling a drop. I'd been practising since last night and I'd normally be thrilled at how quickly I'd mastered the spell, but I wouldn't get a second chance if I spilled the whole thing. No pressure, Blair.

I secured the lid on the bottle, put the potion in my pocket and left for the lake.

The town was deserted at this hour in the morning, and nobody accosted me as I flew through the cobbled streets. It was too early for the High Fliers to be out, and the lake was silent, reflecting the dappled sunlight.

As I neared the shore, I spotted a siren swimming in the shallows. Recognising her as the same siren I'd spoken to after Terrence's death, I moved closer until I stood inches from the lake's edge.

"Hey," I called to her, and she flipped over on the spot, splashing me with lake water. "Wait, don't swim off. I want to talk to you for a minute."

"What about?" She floated closer to shore, propping her elbows on the bank.

"Did you see what happened yesterday? When that High Flier fell into the water?"

A moment's hesitation. "No."

Lie.

"Look, you can tell me. I'm not going to report you." *Unless you committed the crime, that is.* "What did you see?"

"I saw her fall off her broom." She fidgeted. "They're always doing it. I forget how easily humans can drown."

True. "You weren't anywhere near her, were you?"

"No…" She broke off, her gaze dropping. "I *was,* and I know what you're going to say, but I wasn't singing. I can't sing."

Lie.

I blinked at her. Of all the lies to tell, why pick that one? "You… can't sing?"

She winced. "I *can,* but I don't like to sing. I'm out of tune on every note. The others laugh at me whenever they hear me."

True. Huh. I'd never have expected to run into a siren who couldn't sing in tune. It must be demoralising, considering bewitching humans with their beautiful singing was their trademark.

She looked up, her eyes widening. I turned around, seeing a winged shape approaching in the distance. Make that three of them. Oh, no. The gargoyles were coming.

The siren dove underwater, leaving me standing on the shore. Hovering around here alone made *me* look guilty, and if I went looking for the elf, I might bring the gargoyles after both of us. If he was even visible, let alone sober.

I snapped my fingers to switch into fairy mode, then again to turn myself invisible. Hoping they hadn't seen me in the seconds before I vanished, I flew over the lake to avoid being caught in the air currents from the gargoyles' massive wings. I flew high, admiring the glitter of the sun in the water like fractured glass.

Then I spotted someone approaching the lake from the woods. Not a gargoyle, but a human. Annabel.

I halted in mid-air and watched her walk up the path. She must have come out of the woods. Was she planning to make up with Bracken? If she was, and the police caught her hanging around, they might *both* get arrested. I hovered on the spot, debating whether to risk approaching her.

Annabel looked at the water for a moment, then turned and ducked back into the woods. The gargoyles couldn't fly in there, and besides, their attention was on the water. If I flew faster than she walked, maybe I could see if she'd left any clues at her cottage. Like who'd been helping her with her newly discovered powers. Something was definitely fishy there, but I was living proof that someone could develop magical skills as an adult. Maybe I should just *ask* her outright and hope she didn't bite my head off for it.

I flew into the woods, then halted behind a tree, glad of my invisible state. Annabel had stopped walking to speak to two elves—Bramble and Twig. While they spoke too quietly for me to hear, her body language showed agitation. I flew closer, moving as silently as possible. Before I caught up, they parted, Annabel taking the path back towards her house. The elves, meanwhile, headed down a slope leading deeper into the woods.

I remained still, mentally flipping a coin, then followed

the elves down the slope. Before they reached the bottom, they turned around, narrowing their eyes.

"Who's there?" Twig demanded.

Ah. They knew glamour, and something had given me away. Hoping Annabel was too far away to hear, I landed in front of them, turning visible.

"Blair Wilkes," Bramble said. "Come to tell the king about your progress?"

"Not yet," I said. "What were you talking to Annabel about?"

"None of your concern, human."

I resisted the impulse to roll my eyes. "Isn't her ex-boyfriend the person I'm meant to be defending from a potential murder accusation? Assuming they actually catch him." Steve would never think to look behind the falls, but at some point my lies would catch up with me.

"Are you considering betraying our king, Blair Wilkes?" asked Bramble.

"I can't prove Bracken is innocent if he doesn't act it," I told them. "You know he was firing off magical lightning bolts at the exact time the second victim fell off her broom, right?"

I didn't add that he'd also thrown up on his shoes and passed out in front of Nathan's family. Not to mention his invisibility trick. At this point, I just wanted to know if he was guilty. The rest could wait.

"The second death was undoubtedly an accident," Twig growled. "The first was murder, but not by him."

"I'd be happy to defend him if he cooperated with me," I said. "He can't even remember if he hit Laurie's broomstick or not. How am I supposed to defend someone who doesn't remember if they're innocent?"

"He did not murder anyone," he said stubbornly.

True... or so *he* believed. "Has he said anything coherent to either of you?" I asked. "You're more likely to be able to get through to him than I am. You must know that."

"He has said nothing," Bramble growled. "I'd advise you to hurry and keep your word, Blair."

And in a blink, both elves were gone. Worse, I'd lost track of Annabel, and I hadn't checked the time since before I'd glamoured myself.

Oh, no.

———

By the time I got to work, nine o'clock had long passed by. As I slipped into the office, Rob greeted me with his big ridiculous werewolf smile. "Hey, Blair. Rough night?"

I'd thought I looked more windswept than hungover. "No, I slept through my alarm."

Anyone who knew about Sky's existence would know that for a blatant lie. That cat was the most effective alarm clock I'd ever had. Still, I'd rather be chastened for drinking on a weekday than hiding information on a potential murder suspect from the police.

I hadn't even made it to the coffee machine when Veronica came into the office. "Blair, a word, please."

I left the coffee machine and padded after the boss to her office behind the reception area.

Veronica's office changed its decor depending on her mood. Today, it was set out like a beach, complete with deck chairs instead of regular office chairs.

"Sorry I'm late again," I said, sitting in the deck chair. It was a little disconcerting looking up at the boss from a half-lying position, so I perched on the end instead. "I had a rough weekend. I was by the lake when Laurie—the High Flier—fell in and drowned."

"Oh, I'm sorry to hear that," she said, bushing sand off her desk. "Terrible tragedy. Those High Fliers take too many risks. Of course, broomsticks carry their own hazards… I apologise. You're learning to ride one yourself, Madame Grey tells me."

"Yeah, I am," I said. "It's not going great. Maybe now's not the best time to learn, but I have to fulfil one 'other' witch skill to pass my Grade Three witch exams."

"I suppose it's never a bad idea to have an escape strategy," she said. "From those hunters, for instance."

Oh. She must have heard about Nathan's family. "I don't know, I think I prefer using the Seven Millimetre Boots."

"Did you know those boots have an expiry date?" she asked. "Like all spells, they decay with time."

"I didn't know that," I said. "Uh, I'm sorry for being late for work, anyway. I know I haven't been on top of things lately."

She waved a hand. "You found our fourth team member. That's taken a huge weight off our schedules. And when you've mastered a broomstick, even more opportunities will open to you."

I doubt it. When I was done with the exam, I'd never touch a broom again. What with the chaotic weekend I'd had, I'd forgotten my broom classes altogether. But summer was ticking away, and if I didn't pass my exam by the time the holidays finished, I might end up stuck at the grade of a six-year-old forever.

———

When the workday finished, I headed to my flying lesson. After the events of the weekend, the last thing I wanted was to take to the skies, but Veronica's words had reminded me how little time I had left before my exam.

"I can do this," I muttered to myself as I walked to the witch's headquarters. "I can—"

The door swung open and I jumped back to avoid being hit in the face. Helen came out, carrying two broomsticks. "Sorry, Blair. Didn't see you there."

"Is today's lesson somewhere else?" I asked, eyeing the broomsticks. *Please not a public setting. Or the academy.*

"Oh, I've had to cancel the class," Helen said. "We're testing all the covens' broomsticks for jinxes down at the lake. Want to help?"

"Jinxes?" I echoed. "I thought you can't put a spell on a broomstick."

"You can, but not easily," said Helen. "Usually it's done before the broom is even in the air. We want to cover all bases.

"You think someone did that to Laurie's broom?"

It seemed unlikely. The sabotage, if that's what it was, had most likely taken place at the lake, not beforehand. Still, I'd been waiting for a chance to speak to Bracken. Maybe I'd get to visit him while the others were testing the brooms for jinxes.

When we reached the lakeside, it was to find that Helen and several other witches had laid out dozens of broomsticks on the grass.

"It's a simple anti-jinx spell." Helen held out her wand over the nearest broom and waved it. A flash of light went off, and the broom rolled over on the spot. "Want to try?"

"Sure." I moved to the next broom, drawing my wand. Helen ducked as glitter shot from the wand's end.

"Ah." I dropped my head, flushing. "Sorry. I haven't done that for a while."

Being close to the lake again set my nerves on edge. I was certain we were wasting our time testing the brooms for sabotage when the killer had more likely been in, or near, the lake itself. The High Fliers fell off their brooms all the time and were fine.

I copied Helen's spell, but my mind was elsewhere. I still had the memory potion, and it felt like Bracken was our only chance to get to the truth. On the other hand, there was also Annabel to consider. What had she and the elves been discussing? She might not like me, but if Bracken wasn't available to talk to, she might be easier to convince.

———

In the end, the gargoyles made up my mind for me. Before we'd finished testing the first set of brooms, a flock of them appeared overhead. I didn't know what they were looking for, but I'd bet Bracken had glamoured himself invisible at the sight of them. I helped Helen carry armfuls of broomsticks back and forth from the witches' place far past my allotted lesson time, but after an hour and a half, the gargoyles were still flying above the lake.

After our third trip back, my patience was growing thin. Seeing the others had the rest of the broomsticks in hand, I went into the forest to avoid Helen roping me into helping with anything else. Then I turned invisible and flew down the path towards Annabel's house. I didn't think she'd be pleased if I admitted I'd seen her talking to the elves before, but I was curious about what they'd said. Had they been discussing Bracken's reaction to their breakup? Maybe if she helped him, I wouldn't have to trick him into answering my questions. Thanks to the elf's disappearing act, she wasn't known to be linked to the suspects, so the gargoyles ought to leave her alone.

When I knocked, Annabel opened the door, scowling at me. "What do you mean by tattling on me to my grandmother?"

Oh. Ava must have told her. "I didn't know you hadn't already spoken to her about developing the seeing ability. I thought, I don't know, that you'd want guidance."

"Can you imagine her trying to teach me?" She shook her head. "She can't tell her left hand from her right one."

"Why not tell her, though?" I asked. "Even if she couldn't teach you, she could offer advice, right?"

"Have you ever heard a word of her advice?" she said. "No, I didn't tell her. She had enough of an issue with me dating Bracken. I didn't need to hear her gloating."

"Sorry," I said. "But you loved him, right?"

"Of course." She choked on the words. "Of course I do. But I got never-ending crap from everyone else."

"Did he seem bothered, though?" I asked. "If it didn't bother him that people were judgemental of the two of you, then he wouldn't have had reason to end it, would he?"

"I'm never going to know that now, am I?" She sniffed. "I wrecked things. If my grandmother hadn't given me that blasted crystal ball to begin with…"

I blinked. "She gave it to you?"

She dabbed her eyes. "There was a leak in the attic the other week, so I went up there to check it out and found her old crystal ball. I'd forgotten I put it up there, to be honest. It's been in the family for generations. Anyway, I looked into it, and… and I saw us breaking it off."

Her words rang true, but that couldn't be all there was to it. Still, whatever she'd seen in the crystal ball was her own business, after all.

"He still seems pretty torn up about the whole thing," I said to her. "I think he'd be willing to give another shot."

She flinched. "Don't say that. It's too late. It's over."

"Only if you both want it to be."

Be quiet, Blair. I was hardly qualified to give anyone relationship advice, considering what a monumental mess of things I'd made of my meeting with Nathan's family—*both* times. But I still couldn't help wondering if there'd been more to the breakup than a simple vision.

Annabel sighed. "Why am I even talking to you, Blair? You really stirred my grandmother up. She won't stop talking about you."

"I didn't mean to butt in. It's just that Bracken was by the lake when Laurie drowned, and he's too addled to have seen what happened. But he might be the only witness."

"Laurie?" she echoed. "Who?"

"A High Flier," I said. "Have you seen him since then?"

"What do you think?" She ended on a sob and closed the door. I waited, but she didn't open it again.

So much for that. I backed away and my foot caught on a piece of paper wedged under the doorstep. The flier said, *Violet Layne, fortune-teller.*

A fortune-teller? I'd thought Ava was the town's only living seer. Had Annabel met with this Violet Lane?

Maybe she might offer an insight into the sight that old Ava couldn't. I slipped the flier into my pocket and left the cottage behind.

———

"A new seer?" Alissa asked, reading the leaflet. "Never heard of her. I don't know if Ava has either, but she's been acting out today."

I petted Sky, who'd sprawled out next to me on the sofa. It was amazing how such a small cat could take up so much space. "I hope I didn't upset her by telling her about Annabel's and Bracken's breakup."

"It might get her prepared for Bracken's eventual arrest," she said. "Did you give him the potion?"

"Nope." I heaved a sigh. "Helen had me carrying broomsticks around for over an hour and then the gargoyles showed up. The High Fliers asked to have all their brooms tested for jinxes, because they think someone might have damaged Laurie's broom. I can't tell them otherwise without admitting I saw that pesky elf glamour himself invisible."

"But you're sure he didn't do it?"

"Nope, unfortunately." I took the flier back from her. "The issue isn't with the brooms, it's with whoever was nearby when she was flying. I spoke to the same siren who knew Terrence again, but she claims she never uses her siren's song ability because she can't sing in tune. And of course there's Bracken, but I think he needs to sober up or take that potion before he'll tell us anything useful."

"Which means dodging the gargoyles." She nodded. "I'm surprised they haven't found him yet, but I bet they never thought to check behind the falls. Did Helen find anything wrong with the brooms?"

"Nope," I said. "It was a waste of time. I heard those brooms are pretty much impervious to magic anyway, but I don't know if elf magic is an exception. Elves and fairies aren't exactly the same. I guess I could borrow a broomstick and see if I can use magic on it, but I can't shoot magic lightning, and I'm good at making brooms fall out of the air without the need for magic."

"Ha," said Alissa. "Don't give up on the potion too soon, though. It expires within a month."

"Good to know," I said. "Is it too late to visit the seer, do you think?"

"The flier says she's open from noon until midnight. Because the moonlight helps her visions, apparently." She gave an eye-roll. "Sounds like another Ava, to be honest."

"It's worth a shot," I said.

11

———

Violet Layne occupied the once empty shop next to the Enchantment Emporium, the best-known store of miscellaneous objects in the town. The seer's place, however, looked empty, with no visible traces of any inhabitants behind the dusty glass window. But the crooked sign above the door claiming this place belonged to 'Violet Layne, Seer Extraordinaire' matched the elaborate flourish on the leaflet I'd found at Annabel's place.

I opened the door, to the sound of a tinkling bell.

A woman of around Rita's age sat behind a desk, her long dark curly hair bouncing past her shoulders. She had medium brown skin, dark eyes, and wore a long black robe like a scholar. In front of her was a giant crystal ball, bigger than my head. Its planes reflected the small, dusty room back at me. Just in case there was any ambiguity that I'd walked into a seer's shop. Maybe this was a mistake. I was too tired and grumpy to pretend to be interested in fortune-telling.

She followed my line of sight. "You'd be surprised how often people forget what they came in for. I think it's the crystal ball that confuses them."

"Why? If you see a crystal ball, you don't immediately think you're walking into a bank. Not in my experience, anyway."

"You never know," she said. "A lot of people don't want to see what lies ahead."

"I would assume they do if they walk into a shop with a giant sign saying 'Seer Extraordinaire' above the door."

I wondered if I'd gone too far, but she laughed. "I don't need to see to know you're a piece of work, Blair Wilkes. I did wonder if you'd be paying me a visit."

"Do you say that to every customer or just the ones whose names you know?"

"I saw you in here, Blair." She waved a hand at the crystal ball. "Besides, there's nobody in town who *doesn't* know who you are."

"Aren't you new in town?" I said. "I mean, the vampires said there weren't any practising seers in Fairy Falls a few weeks ago. And this shop was empty the last time I came here."

"Vampires." She wrinkled her brow. "Unpleasant creatures. Did you know they can't be seen in crystal balls at all?"

"Really?" My gaze flicked to the glass. "You do fortune-telling for people? Is it as popular here as it is in the normal world?"

Violet Layne wasn't what I'd expected. I'd thought she'd be a little like Ava but with less of the unpredictability factor. Then again, the vampires already had the role of 'cryptic and annoying mysterious elder' filled. She wasn't a mind-reader, but there was a little similarity there, except she could peek into my future rather than my deepest thoughts. Assuming I believed her visions were real.

"Oh, yes, I read people's fortunes," she said. "Yes, it always bewildered me, the normals' fascination with knowing what lies ahead and what is to come. They're not so different from us, Blair. I suppose it's easier to feel prepared for the future if you believe you know how it will play out."

"So you're saying—it's not real?" I asked. "I mean, it doesn't necessarily have to play out the way you think it does?"

"The future is rarely so straightforward," Violet said. "The sight arrives in ambiguous glimpses if at all."

"That doesn't sound like a reliable way to make a living either," I said before I could stop myself. "Unless you don't tell all your customers, *well, it* might *come true, might not, who knows?*"

"There's no need," she said mildly. "Most will leap on anything I tell them. It's better to have an imperfect glimpse than nothing, in their eyes. Few seers have enough of the gift to be able to make an *honest* living out of it. I knew one who lived in the normal world, and the only thing he was able to see was if the bus was going to be late. Every time he looked into a crystal ball, that's all he saw. Often after he'd *already* missed the bus."

"Yeah, that's not much help," I said. "Do seers ever see useful visions?"

"That would depend on your definition of 'useful'."

Thought so. Perhaps Madame Grey had good reason to think of seeing as a wishy-washy form of magic with little practical use.

"In the normal world, fortune-tellers tend to make predictions like 'you'll meet a handsome stranger in a week' or 'you're going to get a job promotion soon'," I said. "It's generally pretty vague. Is magical fortune-telling more specific?"

"Sometimes it is," she said. "Sometimes not."

"How often?"

"How long is a broomstick?"

That's no answer. "Isn't broomstick length supposed to be

standardised? I mean, that's what I heard." Specifically, from Helen, when we'd been de-jinxing the brooms by the lake. She'd given me a full lecture on the subject.

She laughed. "There's always a cynic."

I wouldn't say I was *that* cynical. I just found it hard to believe anyone could have predicted the wild ride my life had taken over the last few months.

"Is it possible to teach someone to see who doesn't have the gift?" I asked.

"Seeing is known for skipping generations," said Violet. "It's rare even in seer families."

"Have you met any others?" I asked. "Here, in Fairy Falls?"

"Here? No. I was under the impression there weren't any."

True. So she hadn't met Annabel, after all. "You moved here recently. Did you see Madame Grey?"

"I did," she confirmed. "Madame Grey gave me permission to set up shop here. I'm still unpacking the furniture."

That'd explain why the crystal ball was the only item on display in the room. I glanced at its glassy surface again, seeing nothing but greyish fog. "If someone without the gift looks into a crystal ball, can they develop the ability to see?"

"Think you might have a trace of the seer gift, love?"

"I don't think so." I had enough weird powers without adding being able to see the future on top of it.

"Your powers aren't that far removed from seeing and its related talents," she mused. "Want to give it a go? This is all free of charge. You interest me, and that's worth any payment, Blair Wilkes."

True. She'd told the truth with every word so far and hadn't tried to deceive me. Though someone who told fortunes for a living was probably careful what they said most of the time.

I turned back to the crystal ball. Its surface had gone murky, smoke swirling below the surface. I crouched to get a better view. It was like looking at clouds in the sky—easy to imagine seeing shapes there, more difficult to know if I was just imagining them. A prickle ran between my shoulder blades.

"See anything?" she asked.

"No, but I feel... odd." My head swam, and the murky smoke didn't help. I couldn't put my finger on it, but the smoke dulled my senses in a way I couldn't explain.

My throat went tight, and I jerked my head back. "What was that?"

"That," she said, "was the price of seeing. No other magic works when it comes into contact with a crystal ball. Yes, not even your truth-sensing power."

It never felt like that before. I'd had my power briefly blocked, but never for a long time, and I'd never felt the sensation of it actively being shut off. Shivers ran down my arms. "I didn't see anything in there," I said. "Unless it means there's going to be a storm, which there probably is."

She gave a laugh. "Well, if you didn't see anything in there, it doesn't look like your talents tend towards seeing. Pity. I would have liked to witness a new seer develop their skills. New seers find their skills are in high demand. You could rake in a fortune."

No thanks. Being a fairy witch already brought me more than enough unwanted attention.

"What about prophetic dreams?" I asked. "Or dreams about the past? I didn't remember any of my life before I was adopted until I moved here. Now I'm having weird dreams about it." I hadn't had one for a while, but I did wonder.

"Describe them."

"Usually I'm flying," I said. "Over the countryside. I thought I might be remembering being here before I was sent into the normal world."

"That doesn't sound like seeing." She sounded disappointed. "Seeing involves clarity. It doesn't mean you're clear about the meaning, but there is never any doubt about what the person is seeing."

"That's not really clear, is it?" I had the inkling that arguing with a seer about clarity was a recipe for disaster. "Have you ever mentored anyone?"

"Mentor? Me? This is not an art that can be taught, Blair."

"But you just said you wanted to mentor me if I had the skill," I pointed out.

"Oh, I meant I'd give you a few tips. Seeing can only be learned from seeing, if you know what I mean."

"I don't think I do." It still sounded pretty wishy-washy to me. But if she hadn't mentored Annabel, who had? "Where would I go if I wanted to purchase a crystal ball?"

"Next door, of course," she said. "Crystal balls are made from enchanted glass and require a wizard or witch with immense skill to create. The process takes a long time. Rare, tricky magic. Expensive, too. But I have to say, that's not my area of expertise. I look *into* the glass. I don't *create* it. That's the enchanter's job."

"Okay, thanks," I said. "I appreciate you taking the time to talk to me."

She leaned back in her seat. "Oh, feel free to drop by any time. You might not have the skill yourself, but I've no doubt you'll show up in the glass again soon. Any time you want a reading, I'll give you a discount."

"Thanks," I said, though I didn't need a crystal ball to predict another storm of bad luck coming my way. Maybe the clouds indicated what was coming the day of my broomstick exam—which I was still woefully unprepared for.

Violet Layne had never met Annabel, which meant that flier must have been delivered to every address on that street and wasn't directed at her. One theory down.

I left the seer's shop, turned right, and halted in front of the Enchantment Emporium. It stayed open later than the other shops on this street, and its owner was an enchanter—a wizard with unique skills in enchanting objects. Since Gus was the best enchanter in Fairy Falls, maybe he knew who'd created the crystal ball Annabel had inherited from her grandmother.

The Enchantment Emporium was the brightest shop I'd seen in the whole town. The shelves sparkled with permanent lights like Christmas decorations, while the rail-thin owner dressed in a cape made entirely out of small, glittering mirrors. At least my glitter-shedding fairy form wouldn't be out of place in this particular shop.

On cue, Gus appeared in a puff of smoke like a stage magician. I managed not to jump this time. "Hey, Gus. Sorry I'm in here so late…"

"Blair Wilkes," he said, an accusing note to his voice. "What do you mean by not telling me you were a fairy? How dare you."

I blinked. "I didn't know you wanted me to tell you."

We'd only met once before, and it was before my fairy side had been exposed for the world to see. I'd figured most people in town had heard about it by this point unless they were asleep in a coffin.

"Your magic." He waved a hand and a spark appeared, reflected in the mirrors on his coat. "I can do fancy tricks like this, but your magic is a whole different *world*, Blair. I must see a demonstration."

"Uh, why?" I asked. "Just an academic interest?"

"Of course." He moved behind the desk, the mirrors catching the lights and dazzling my eyes. "Fairy magic and witch magic are different spheres. It's a shame those pesky regulations imposed on your witch training will keep you from learning enchantments for a while."

"Enchantments are advanced magic, right?" I asked, in an attempt to steer the topic back on track.

"Very advanced. It requires inventiveness as well as skill, and fairies possess a huge amount of both."

"And elves?" I asked, thinking of the magic lightning.

"Absolutely," Gus said. "It's a pity they rarely partner with witches or wizards. They'll work with humans, but they think our magic is incompatible."

If he didn't know any elves, there was a chance he didn't know if an elf's magical lightning could knock the protective spells off a broomstick. But now the subject had come up... "Do you enchant broomsticks, too?"

"I can," he said. "It's not the most challenging spell. Health and safety guidelines prevent me from doing anything too adventurous. The High Fliers sometimes put in requests for other upgrades, but the council usually shoots them down."

"I can imagine," I said. "So it's not possible to knock someone off a broomstick with a spell?"

"Anything is *possible*, Blair Wilkes," he said. "But my broomsticks are jinx-proof. All of them."

That suggested Laurie hadn't been knocked off at all, but who knew how elf magic worked? Let's face it, the only way to get to the truth was to find a way to sneak around the gargoyles and get that potion to Bracken.

"What about crystal balls?" I asked. "How do you enchant the glass to make it show the future?"

"Have you got a week to listen to the details?" He leaned on the desk, mirrors twinkling. "Enchanted glass is one of the trickiest, most rewarding types of enchantment I can do. I can do basic illusions, that type of thing, but to make a piece of glass reflect the *future*... it takes a great deal of time."

"Uh, has anyone ordered a crystal ball recently? Or asked about them?"

"Ordered? No. If you mean the Seer next door, she

brought her own from outside the town. You spoke to her, right? Did she read your fortune?"

"Not exactly," I said. "Never mind. Thanks for talking to me."

Gus was younger than Ava, which meant it was unlikely that he'd been the one to sell her the crystal ball that she'd given to Annabel. She'd said it'd been in her family for generations, besides.

"Your fairy magic?" He looked at me expectantly. "You promised a demonstration."

"Oh, all right." I snapped the fingers of my right hand, turned into fairy mode, then turned human again. The mirrors on his coat reflected my transformation back at me.

Gus applauded. "Masterful work. A glamour… better than one of my illusions, I think. You could do so much with that power."

"I'm not allowed to use my fairy powers in my witch exams." Which was part of the problem. I'd feel more confident on a broomstick if I had wings, but that would defeat the purpose.

"Really? That's a shame." He tilted his head. "You'd fit in here if you're ever looking for something a little different."

"Thanks, but uh, I like working at Dritch & Co."

What was it with people offering me jobs due to my novelty status? Someone else needed to pull a ridiculous public stunt, or else people would start showing up at Dritch & Co wanting to hire *me*.

My phone started to ring as I left the Enchantment Emporium behind. I expected Alissa but instead found Madame Grey on the other end of the line.

"Oh, hi," I said, surprised. "Is something wrong?"

"Blair," she said. "I have very good news. I managed to get a slot for you to take your Grade Three exams next week before classes start again."

"Did you say… excuse me, did you say next week?"

"Yes, I did. Rita said you already covered all the theory work."

"Uh, yeah, but… but does that include the broomstick exam?"

"You selected that as your extra qualification, didn't you? I have you scheduled for this Saturday."

Five days from now. My stomach lurched. "Oh. I'm not…"

"It'll have to be before winter comes," she said. "This is the best season to fly. Unlike the High Fliers—not to speak ill of the dead—we put safety first."

My throat went dry. I needed much more time, but she had a point about the scheduling.

"Is that the only date?" I asked.

"I'm afraid it is, Blair."

Maybe the tight deadline would cause my broom-flying instincts to kick in. Hey, I could dream. "Okay, I'll do it."

12

Focus, Blair.

I stood on the grassy hill in front of the lake beside the broomstick I'd borrowed from the store cupboard, fighting an inexplicable wave of nervousness. This was ridiculous. I'd failed at using a wand at first, too. This would be no different. Besides, what kind of witch couldn't fly a broomstick?

Helen was busy teaching a class at the academy, which left me with no choice but to practise alone. Picking a spot close to the lake felt like tempting fate, but there were few open spaces within the town's boundaries and even fewer where there'd be no witnesses. The High Fliers weren't practising today, so I'd at least have a clear path to fly without crashing into anyone or knocking them out with my broomstick. No gargoyles had shown up either, giving me no excuses not to do my best.

The pressure was on. If I wanted to pass my exam, I needed to get the hang of flight.

"Go time, Blair," I muttered. "You, Mr Broomstick, are going to behave."

I could see Sky's judgemental face in the corner of my eye as I scolded the broom. There was the slight possibility that I was cracking up, but if it took a stern talking-to to get my broomstick to behave, so be it. Standing in position, I tapped the broom's end firmly. I didn't think it was my glamour that was the problem, but something else causing the broom to reject me. Aside from lack of confidence and being humiliated in front of small children, that is.

The broom rose into the air, carrying me with it. Gripping the broomstick between my knees, I took flight, trying to pretend I was using my wings or boots instead. I hadn't worn my boots today, wondering if they might be part of the reason the broom didn't want me to stay airborne. My wings, I couldn't do anything about, but if I stayed in human mode, hopefully it wouldn't matter.

I kept rising into the air, higher, higher. Hey, I was doing it!

The broom dipped forwards. I grabbed the end, fighting for control. My hands grasped the end, and the broom rocked and steadied. Then it dropped again. If I let go and got my wings out, I'd fall off.

"Stop it!" I yelled at the broomstick. "Stop doing that."

The broom tilted to the side, causing me to overbalance. I landed flat on my back on the grass. The broom drifted to land beside me.

"Thanks," I said to it. "What's the issue?"

Taking off wasn't the problem. I just lost focus easily when I was in mid-air, which wasn't surprising, given that my head was as clouded as that bloody crystal ball. Who even cared about broomsticks? Two people had died right nearby, and the elf was nowhere in sight. I'd walked here through the woods and peered down at the falls, but no elves had come out. The day was overcast, which explained why nobody else was around, but I'd heard whispers that the High Fliers had put their summer event on hold until they found out if Laurie had been murdered.

I mounted the broom again. This time I lasted four seconds before it pitched forward, throwing me off the end. I sighed and snapped into fairy mode, getting back on the broomstick. This time was even worse. I was barely in the air when a wind current caught my wings from behind, sending me flying head over heels. I crash-landed on my back once again, my wings protesting at the impact.

Wait. I got to my feet, twitching my wings. The air current had hit me from behind. Were the wings somehow making it harder for me to stay on the broomstick? If the wind blew from behind and caught my wings, it was pretty much a given that the broom would tip forwards and throw me off. Maybe I needed to face the other way.

I turned the broom around, wings still out, and mounted. Taking in a breath, I pulled the broom into position and tapped the end with my wand. The air current hit from the front this time, tugging on my wings and threatening to send me flying *back* off the broom and not forwards. I gripped harder, flying slightly to the left. If I flew at a slight angle, I could avoid the wind catching my wings and blowing me off course. I wasn't sure the exam's rules would allow lopsided flying, but now I knew what the problem was.

The broom tipped. I fell off, landing on my back, and found myself looking up at my cat. Where had he come from?

"Miaow." Sky prodded me in the chest with a paw.

"Sky?" I sat up, brushing grass off my back. "What are you doing here? You never come to the lake. Unless you've found another treasure map?"

"Miaow."

I retrieved the broomstick where it'd fallen onto the grass. "I'm learning to ride a broom, but having wings makes balancing a bit tricky. Want to help me out?"

I positioned the broom between my legs again. With a tap of my wand, I was in the air—and to my complete and utter astonishment, Sky jumped up, perching on the end. The broom dipped forwards and I cringed, but it didn't overbalance this time.

"Are you balancing the broomstick?"

"Miaow."

How had Sky even known to come here? I pulled the broom up a little, expecting it to throw me off. Then I flew forwards. Each time the broom titled, Sky shifted his weight, pushing it back on course. *I'm doing this. I'm really doing this.*

I flew up, then down, aiming to land on the bank. I'd never had a successful landing before, but the broom halted when I steadied it, and I jumped off and landed on my feet.

I punched the air in triumph. Sky remained sitting on the floating broomstick, looking as indifferent as ever. I grinned at him. "Come on, you know that was awesome."

I leapt onto the broom and took flight again, steering over the lake. *At last.* Maybe the presence of a cat on the end of the broom had convinced it that I was a real witch.

I flew over the lake again and back to shore, elated. Now all I needed was to find the elf. I'd peeked behind the waterfall earlier, but he might have been glamoured and hiding. Or he'd found a new hiding place. I didn't *think* he'd have gone home to the other elves, but if he had, perhaps there'd be no need to confront him at all. They wouldn't hide a criminal among them, would they? Okay, my dad had hidden from the hunters in the forest, but he was a fairy, not an elf.

I landed at the lake's edge and bounded off the broom into the shallows, splashing both of us in the process. Sky hopped off the broom and shook himself, giving me a reproachful look.

"I rode a broomstick," I told him. "We both did. Isn't that great?"

"Miaow."

"All right, let's find our misfit elf."

Sky padded alongside me. He kept stopping and staring into the trees, his fur standing on end, but whenever I looked among the bushes, there was nobody there.

Since I didn't have my boots, I used my wings instead, leaving the broomstick at the top of the slope to avoid having to carry it downhill. Sky sat beside it, his ears twitching.

"I'll just be a minute," I told him, taking flight towards the falls.

Once again, I landed beside the crashing water. I peered into the small cave but saw no signs of the elf's presence. Even the bottles had gone.

"Hey," I said, spotting the merman splashing in the river. "Hey, where's Bracken?"

"He left," he said, his expression downcast. "This morning. He went into the forest."

Oh, no. That's what I got for dawdling. He must have moved his lair elsewhere. Or joined the other elves again. Maybe he'd reconciled with them, but I doubted it. Most likely, the other elves had had enough of him making a public nuisance of himself and dragged him into the forest themselves before he got arrested.

I re-joined Sky at the top of the slope. "He's gone," I told the cat. "Are you up for a walk in the woods?"

"Miaow." Sky's ears twitched, but he padded after me down the woodland path.

Propping my broomstick on my shoulder High Flier-style, I walked on, calling for the pixie. I'd seen no signs of him all week either, which was unusual. Coupled with his odd behaviour when I'd met Nathan's family, I wasn't feeling particularly well-disposed towards him, but he was my quickest route to the elves without intentional trespassing.

"Miaow," Sky said from behind me.

I turned to the little cat. "Can you find the elves in here? You don't have to go off alone if you don't want to."

"Miaow." He darted to my side, weaving around my legs and between my feet.

"Whoa," I said. "What is it?"

Footsteps came from the path. I froze, then relaxed when I saw the huge hulking form of Donovan of the wolf pack.

Wait. Maybe I shouldn't relax. I'd accidentally hired his nephew as our newest team member while knowing full well how much he despised Dritch & Co, but I'd forgotten all that in the wake of the more recent drama.

Chief Donovan narrowed his eyes at me. "Blair Wilkes."

"Oh, hey," I said to him. It wasn't any use pretending not to see a huge blond dude who could turn into a wolf. He was almost as conspicuous as I was in full fairy guise. "I was just walking with my cat."

Sky wound around my legs, hissing. I hoped he wouldn't turn into his monster glamour and start a fight.

"You look like you're interfering in something again," said Chief Donovan. "What do you mean by corrupting my nephew?"

I couldn't say I hadn't seen it coming. "I didn't corrupt him. He applied to work at my office and passed the interview. None of the other candidates did, so my boss decided to hire him. Take it up with her if you have a problem, not me."

His mouth turned down at the corners. "Rob never showed the slightest interest in recruiting... whatever it is you do. He applied as a joke, nothing more."

"Actually, he's pretty good at it. Ask Veronica."

"If you bring any of your atrocious luck anywhere near my pack, Blair Wilkes, then I will take my family and move as far away from you as possible."

Atrocious luck? Maybe that's what I needed—a lucky latte. Though last time I'd tried that, it'd backfired horribly. Like seeing the future, it was impossible to plan for every possible scenario. You just had to do the best with what you had.

I gave him a smile. "If anything, I think it's a good thing that he and Callie are working closely with the other paranormals. If they enjoy the work and want to stay, what's the big deal? It's not like they're out hunting wild… er, unicorns." I'd almost referenced the hunters but caught myself at the last second.

"You have a knack for trouble, Blair. Don't deny it."

"Don't worry, I wasn't going to," I said. "It's still Rob's choice, and he likes working at our office."

There was no point in denying that Callie had met with a fair few accidents when I was around, but I hadn't actually been responsible for any of them. And Rob's presence had improved things at Dritch & Co dramatically. I'd never thought I'd be glad to have any more of Chief Donovan's relatives in my immediate presence, but I should have learnt to expect the unexpected from the paranormal world by now. It wasn't as simple or black-and-white as the hunters believed it to be. Maybe the chief and I would never be BFFs, but it'd be nice to bury any past animosity between us.

"What are you doing in this part of the woods, anyway?" I asked, when he didn't respond. "It's witch territory."

Not elf territory, thank goodness, but I'd never seen the werewolves' chief wandering around here before. I'd assumed he stuck to the shifters' areas of the woods.

He straightened himself upright. "I was having a word with Madame Grey about the new jail conditions."

"What about them?"

"They're not suitable for shifters," he said. "Too much silver. Too much like…" He paused, nostrils flaring. "Hunters. Is one of them with you?"

"Hunters? Nope. If you mean Nathan, not him either." I hadn't heard from him since the weekend.

"No." He inhaled. "There are humans in here."

"Er, yeah, I know, I am one."

Without another word, Chief Donovan turned around and disappeared into the trees.

Sky unwound himself from my legs. "Miaow."

"Relax, he won't do anything to either of us," I muttered to him. "He's quite reasonable when the hunters aren't around. I just have a knack for touching a nerve with him. Don't know what he meant by the hunters, though. I thought Nathan's family left." My heart fluttered uneasily.

Sky's fur stood on end and he hissed. "Miaow."

"Is there someone else out there?"

I carried on walking down the path, despite Sky's warning hiss. The murmur of voices reached my ears, and a moment later, I spotted two small, pointy-eared figures. Bramble and Twig.

"Come to follow us, have you, Blair Wilkes?" Bramble said.

"I didn't know you were here." Why was everyone on the witches' territory today? "Did you know where Bracken went? Is he with you?"

"With any luck," he growled. "We're in the process of convincing the king to join us on our journey to seek a new place to hide outside the woods."

I blinked. "What? You're leaving? Why?"

"Times change," said Twig. "I do not think the forest is the place for us any longer."

"Then—where? Is Bracken already gone?"

"Bracken is lost," he said. "He's gone, but he's not with us."

"So he ran off and you want to do the same?" Oh, no. If he'd left town, I could wave goodbye to any chance of getting to the truth about the murders. "I can't prove his innocence to the police if he isn't here."

"Ever since that beast showed up, the forest hasn't felt the same," said Twig. "Something has changed. An ill wind, as the humans say."

So they sensed whatever was in the woods, too. Or *who*ever. I wished I'd texted Nathan. He'd warned me enough times about going into the woods alone. At least I had my cat with me.

"Maybe it's because you rejected Bracken's relationship with Annabel?" I asked. "You must know his feelings won't change just because you think they should."

"That's not your place to say, human."

"Nor is it yours." I couldn't believe the elf had *gone*. He must have left before I'd arrived at the lake, so he'd be beyond the town's boundaries by now. Or maybe lost in the woods. Given the state of him, who knew? "He was happy with Annabel and you ruined it. How is this a good thing for anyone?"

"It's in the past," Bramble growled. "As Fairy Falls will be, when I convince the king."

"Look, you don't have to leave." I might not *like* him, but I couldn't imagine the forest without the elves there. "How do you know the king wouldn't just tell you that you're being ridiculous? Have you told *him* where Bracken is?"

Bramble didn't say anything. Hang on a minute. "Are you trying to cover your tracks rather than admit you drove him out?"

The faintest flush on his pale, pointed face betrayed his guilt. "No."

Lie.

I rolled my eyes. "Really? I thought your people didn't like to lie."

"That's *your* people, Blair Wilkes," he growled. "*Mine* will do everything to protect our own."

"Except if they date humans, apparently," I said. "I saw you two talking to Annabel the other day. What were you doing, trying to persuade her to leave? I know you didn't want them to stay together."

"It's not natural," Twig growled. "Humans will never understand our ways."

"Says who? I doubt the king will uproot all of the other elves from the forest because one of you did a runner. How do you know he's not lost in the woods himself?"

"Perhaps he is," said Twig, "but we've been unable to find him. He refused to listen to any of our attempts to persuade him to come back. I hoped Annabel would talk some sense into him, but—"

"But she doesn't want to talk to him," I guessed. "Because she broke up with him. Have you visited her before?"

"No."

Lie. From Bramble's face, he knew I'd backed him into a corner. He couldn't lie without me knowing in an instant.

"Was it you who caused them to break up?" I asked the two elves. "Annabel couldn't see the future at all until she went into the attic and found the crystal ball. She said she'd forgotten the crystal ball was even there until a leak in the roof forced her to go up there. Seems a weird coincidence, huh?"

The two of them were as transparent as non-enchanted glass. Somehow, the elves had messed with her crystal ball so it'd show her breaking up with Bracken.

"That girl was unsuited to set foot in our forest," mumbled Twig.

"For what, being human?" I said. "You know breaking and entering is a crime, right? And so is using your magic on someone's property."

"It was an error in judgement," said Twig.

"It was necessary," Bramble interjected. "We are not made to mingle with humans. Work and cooperate with them, yes, but not *marry*."

The penny dropped. "He was going to propose to her," I said. "Or the other way around. Right?"

The two elves must have worked out that Annabel and Bracken were serious enough to consider a public announcement of their relationship, despite the ridicule they'd faced. I respected Annabel even more now. I needed to tell her the truth, but would she believe the elves would sabotage her if they wouldn't admit to it?

"That's not a nice thing to do," I told them. "You ruined Bracken's life, and now two people are dead and he's too addled to help us find out who did it."

Assuming he didn't do it himself.

"Not only Bracken. You hurt Annabel as badly as you hurt him," I added, when neither of them responded. "I know you play by different rules to the humans, but she did absolutely nothing to you and you tried to ruin her life."

Bramble flushed. "It was for the best," he said, but his voice was less heated than before. More ashamed.

I pushed harder. "You don't have to do this," I said. "Maybe it won't work out between those two, but it's not for you to decide. Not to mention there are two sets of people who lost someone they loved and they might never get closure if I don't find and question Bracken. Even if you won't reconsider leaving, can you at least tell me where he went?"

Twig turned around, pointing. "He was heading north along the path, last I saw."

"So he left town." I'd have to follow, against my better judgement. "All right. I'm going to find him, and I really hope you'll reconsider asking your king to leave town. Not that I'd object to *you* leaving, but that's the coward's way out and you know it."

Bramble cleared his throat. "I will reconsider, Blair Wilkes."

Wow. Had I got through to the stubborn elf? Maybe the seer was right. People were searching for a sign, for someone to tell them what to do. I was pretty sure Annabel and Bracken should never have split up. And if I could catch him, perhaps I could help them both.

Even if one of them had to spend their life behind bars.

I turned to Sky. "Let's find him," I said. "Do you know the way?"

"Miaow." His fur bristled, indicating he wasn't keen on the idea of going any further into the woods, but it'd get dark in a few hours. I'd need to be quick.

Sky took the lead down the path. We'd have to avoid shifter territory, which occupied the north of the forest, but the path directly alongside the lake was neutral territory all the way until it ended at the town's border, near the part of the lake furthest from Fairy Falls. I walked until I reached the top of the slope, then took flight above the lake.

Sky didn't follow, but every time I flew to a new stretch of forest to check my bearings, he was there, reliable and loyal. Even if I might be a mediocre witch, I'd lucked out in the familiar department.

I watched the still waters as I flew over the lake, scanning the shores for any signs of the elf. I hoped he hadn't gone into shifter territory, but chances were, he was too drunk to know the boundaries.

I halted in mid-air. There *was* someone standing outside the woods on the north of the lake, but it wasn't an elf. It was a human.

Nathan's father.

13

Mr Harker looked at me as I landed. There was no way I could hide myself—or my fairy wings.

Or Sky, who appeared in front of my legs, hissing at the top of his lungs.

I tried a smile. "Nice day for a walk, isn't it?"

"Don't play the fool with me, Blair. You may have bewitched my son with the innocent act, but I know better. What are you doing this far from town?"

"Looking for an… acquaintance." There was no point in making up an elaborate cover story. It wasn't like he knew the elf, nor would he make the connection unless I referenced the unfortunate incident on our last ill-fated walk by the lake.

"Was this an elf, by any chance?" he said.

Maybe not. How did he know? *He must have seen Bracken coming this way and recognised him.* "Uh—I guess you remember him from the lake."

"I suppose it's true what they say about you."

"Who's 'they'?" Wariness prickled up my spine. I trusted Nathan with my life, but this man was an unknown. And while he didn't scare me as much as his boss, the Inquisitor, something about him set my nerves on edge. What was he even doing here? He couldn't have seen me through the trees, so he couldn't have expected to meet me.

Sky hissed at him again, but he barely spared the little cat a glance.

"I think you should drop the act, Blair. I'm not as easy to fool as some of the other hunters you might have encountered."

No—he wasn't a fool. But that didn't mean I had the faintest clue what'd got him so wound up.

"Act?" I said. "If you're going to tell me to stay away from Nathan, then that's not happening. As for what I did to the other hunters, I'm not sorry I cost Sleepy, Dopey and Grumpy their jobs or sent the hunters packing from town for trying to unseat the council."

"Cost *who* their jobs?" He shook his head. "Blair, I've heard of your exploits, but that's not what I'm referring to. Since it seems you are indeed as slow as you're pretending to be, I mean your fairy nature, of course."

A cold hard pit formed in my stomach. "What, that's why you want me to stay away from Nathan? I might be a fairy, but I grew up human and have no paranormal benchmark to measure myself against. I'm learning as I go, not trying to corrupt anyone. You must know you sound ridiculous. Besides, Nathan's a grown man who can take care of himself."

"He's known for making rash decisions that go against tradition."

I blinked at him. "What, leaving the hunters?"

"Yes. Now my daughter has decided to follow in his footsteps."

Oh. Nathan had told me ages ago that Erin only joined

the hunters to prove to her brothers that she could. I doubted I was in any way responsible for her decision.

"That's her choice, too," I said. "I didn't say a word to her. What's your issue with me? Sure, my cat might have caused an incident at dinner, but it's not like I did anything dangerous or illegal."

His gaze was sharp. "Your family members are known to be criminals and miscreants. It's no big secret, especially to us."

My breath caught. *He knows. Of course he knows.* Blythe's mother never did tell me the details of what my family had supposedly done, but maybe *he* knew.

"I can't have learned to be a criminal mastermind from my family if I've never met them," I pointed out. "Can I?"

"I'm aware of that, Blair, because your mother told me before she died."

His words hung there in the air, weighted, as a long moment passed, seconds stretching out.

"What did you just say?" My voice was a hoarse whisper. "My mum—"

"Told me before she died," he said, his tone dispassionate. "It's more common than you'd expect for criminals like her to turn themselves in. They grow tired of the chase and give into the inevitable. When we found her hideout, she hardly had breath left to tell us that we were to leave you alone, that you weren't part of the paranormal world. Then she passed."

A shard of glass lodged in my throat. I wondered if I was about to cry or shout out, but I felt nothing but cold. Except for my lie-sensing power, telling me unnecessarily that every word he said was true.

"You saw her," I said, my mouth moving on autopilot. "How... how did she die?"

"No doubt one of the enemies she made caught up with her," he said, his tone casual. "Very common among criminal elements. Their friends are as likely to stab them in the back as their enemies are. That's why it's best not to get involved with them."

"I'm not involved with any criminals." My mouth kept moving, though my body was still numb, and the world tilted under my feet as though I stood on the deck of a rocking ship. "My mother—she *died?* Why did nobody tell me?"

"You weren't supposed to be part of this world, Blair," he said. "She said so herself."

Ice slid down my spine. I'd wondered why they'd caught my dad and nobody else, and why he'd come to the forest alone. The odds were never good, no matter how I looked at the situation. But to hear definitive proof from him... *no. It can't be real.*

But he didn't lie.

Which meant one thing: Nathan himself must have known, or at least suspected. Unless his father had never mentioned it, but he'd been there when the hunters had brought my dad into the jail...

Mr Harker stepped away from me. "I have other business here, Blair, so I'll take my leave. But I hope you'll consider my words."

I couldn't *say* a word. *My mum is dead. She's dead.*

If I admitted it, some deep part of me had known from the moment I'd learned she hadn't been seen in town since before my birth. Not even when her own mother—my grandmother—had died. When my dad hadn't responded when I'd asked him if any of my other relatives had survived. If she was alive, he'd have found a way to tell me.

You weren't supposed to be part of this world, Blair.

Maybe he was right. My mother hadn't wanted me to be part of the paranormal world. Even my dad wanted me to leave town. *To protect my life. Not because he thinks I don't belong here.*

It didn't matter what Mr Harker said. He was just another hunter, nothing more.

No… more like another Inquisitor. And while Mr Harker hadn't terrified me as much as Inquisitor Hare had, he'd shattered my world like a crystal ball. I'd bet if I'd seen anything in the glass, it sure wouldn't have shown me *that*.

I sank down onto the grass at the lake's edge, tears streaming down my face. What was I supposed to do with myself now? I shook with sobs, pressing my clenched fists to my eyes as though to shut out the world.

"Miaow," said Sky, nudging my leg.

"What?" I scrubbed my eyes with the back of my hand. "It's not like anyone will miss me if I just stay here all day."

"Miaow!"

"Yes, I know I came here to look for Bracken, but he's probably gone. What does it matter anyway?"

Sky growled. I jumped to my feet as a pair of huge mismatched eyes gleamed from a face of shaggy fur. Sky had put on his monster glamour, his teeth gleaming, his body suddenly the size of a lion.

"There's no need for that, Sky."

"Miaow," he rumbled.

"If anything, you should be chasing off Nathan's dad, not me."

Monster-Sky turned into normal-Sky and licked my hand. I blinked at his abrupt change, twisting around to look over my shoulder. Mr Harker was long gone, but now I thought about it…

"Mr Harker is still here," I told Sky. "Can you tail him, chase him away if necessary? I'll be fine."

I wouldn't, not for a while, but I had a job to do: find the elf. Who knew, maybe he'd found a new place to live that would accept a fairy witch with a criminal family.

No. Fairy Falls is my home. And whatever Mr Harker said, I could still stop Bracken and Annabel from making a mistake they'd both regret forever.

I drew in a breath, wiped the tears away, and walked north.

———

Trailing after a drunken elf was a new low even for me. For a while, I wondered if I'd gone in the wrong direction. There was no sign of the elf, just hills and fields stretching for miles all around me. I'd forgotten just how isolated Fairy Falls was. In the last few months, I'd all but forgotten the world outside.

I didn't want to leave. Nor did I want to give up on Nathan and me. But his father had torn open a raw wound, and when I spotted the elf surrounded by bottles on the hillside. I was more tempted to join him than anything else. Maybe we could set up a community for drunkard elves and fairy witches with criminal relatives.

Bracken looked up at me. "You followed me here? You look different."

"Pretty sure you've seen me as a fairy before." I sat down, tucking my wings against my back. "What's that?" I indicated the bottles.

"Wine."

"Are you willing to share a bottle?" I asked him. "I just found out my mother died."

"Oh, drink away," he slurred. "Everyone dies, or leaves, or forgets." He hiccoughed, tears leaking from his eyes.

I took the bottle he offered. The wine smelled strong enough that I could probably get drunk on it just by inhaling. I closed my eyes, and a tear leaked free. *Stay strong, Blair.* I'd come here for him, not for me.

"Bracken," I said quietly. "I ran into two other elves on the way here. They confessed they tricked you."

"Hmm?" His gaze was on the bottle.

"They tricked you," I repeated. "Bramble and Twig felt threatened by your relationship with Annabel, do you know?"

"Oh, Annabel!" He broke into a fresh flood of sobbing.

"Hang on." I blinked away my own grief. "Annabel never wanted to end it. The other elves tricked her into believing a fake illusion spell they put on her own crystal ball."

He hiccoughed again. "You're a liar, too?"

"No, I'm not," I said. "I do tell little white lies sometimes, but I know when someone else tells the truth. It's my special talent, because I'm half fairy."

"Yes, you have wings," he said, putting the bottle down. "Magic isn't my strong point. All I can do is pointless party tricks like this." Bolts of lightning shot from his hands into the sky.

"Can you show me it again?" I leaned backwards out of range.

When he stood, throwing out more lightning bolts. I pulled the bottle of memory potion from my pocket and swiftly cast the swapping spell. In a heartbeat, the potion's contents switched with the bottle he'd been holding.

Bracken fired one more bolt, fell over, then stumbled back to his nest. He sat down, picked up the wine bottle, and drank heavily. "It doesn't matter what fancy magic tricks I can do… she's gone."

"Did you hear what I said?" I had maybe a few seconds before the potion started working. Alissa had said it was quick-acting but couldn't promise he'd cooperate. The rest was up to me.

"Hmm." His eyes slid closed, then snapped open. "You what? Who tricked me?"

"I'll tell you if you answer a question," I said. "Was it you who knocked Laurie off her broom?"

"No." He spoke with certainty, though his gaze was distant. "I saw her fall."

Truth. He hadn't been responsible for her death. "And Terrence? Did you see what happened to him?"

He stared into space a little more. "No… no, I didn't."

Truth. Finally. But then, who'd killed him?

"Weren't you going to tell me someone tricked me?" he asked.

"The elves used their magic on Annabel's crystal ball to persuade her to end the relationship. She never wanted to break up with you."

His jaw dropped. "What?"

"I'm telling the truth," I said. "She doesn't know yet, but I'm going to make those elves apologise to her if they haven't already. And to you as well. But they won't be able to find you out here. You'll have to come back to the town."

He staggered to his feet. "That's not true. She ended it, she wanted to."

"She didn't want to," I said. "The other *elves* wanted to. I even had them admit it and start grovelling at me. Don't you want to see that?"

"Grovelling at a human? Bramble?" He laughed. "I'd like to see that."

I'd convinced him, but before I got him to speak to Annabel, I should forewarn her. And ask Bramble and Twig to apologise.

"Can you walk back okay?" I asked, hoping Mr Harker was far away by now. At least Sky was on his tail.

"I can walk." He staggered along the path, his steps not quite as uncertain as before. The potion was working its magic—but it wouldn't last forever. And I'd lost my broomstick somewhere on the way. I must have dropped it where I'd run into Nathan's father.

"All right," I said to the elf. "I'll fly behind you."

I flew south, keeping pace with the tottering elf. It was slow going, but better than risking him falling into the lake.

I kept one eye on the shimmering waters, wishing I could forget my own troubles so easily. Tanith Wildflower, my mother… if she was dead, her entire coven likely was, too. Except for Blythe's family. I already knew my maternal grandparents had died, and if my mum had had any siblings, they'd have stayed here. Unless they didn't know I existed or didn't want to get in touch. With Mum gone, that left one surviving member of my immediate family. I understood why Dad wouldn't have wanted to tell me that in a letter. He'd probably been planning to tell me on the solstice when we met face to face.

Tears trickled down my face, dripping into the lake. The water's surface was tranquil. Deceptively calm. While I'd successfully persuaded Bracken to come back with me, I'd only added a new layer to the mystery. But if I got Bracken and Annabel to reconcile, I'd have at least achieved one good thing on what was becoming a serious contender for the worst day of my life so far.

As I flew over the water, I spotted something glittering below the surface. Had the elf been throwing his empty bottles in there?

I dipped down near the shallows. Large shards of broken glass lay scattered, glittering with sunlight. Not the same glass as the elf's bottles. In fact, it looked like… enchanted glass.

Like a crystal ball.

My eyes followed the arrangement of the shards, and certainty slid into me. Annabel must have thrown the crystal ball into the lake in a fit of despair after her vision. I landed beside the shallows and reached out, wincing when the sharp edge of a glass piece nicked my finger.

No wonder the merpeople were avoiding the shallows. Aside from the obvious, that is. But we were miles away from the sites of the two deaths.

I turned over the piece of crystal and felt a familiar odd pressure behind my eyes. The sensation of having my lie-sensing power muted.

Hang on a second. Could they counter *any* witch magic? Including other latent talents?

"That looks like foul play to me," I muttered to myself.

Bracken hadn't known about the crystal ball or his fellow elves' sabotage, and wouldn't truly believe it until they had a change of heart and came clean. He hadn't until I told him—that much was clear. But that meant he couldn't be responsible for its presence in the water.

I slipped the shard of glass into my pocket and flew to join him on the shore. We were closer than I thought to the Fairy Falls, and the main part of the forest I knew.

"Did you see that in the lake?" I asked him, holding up the shattered glass.

He shook his head. "No... that's pretty."

"It's pretty dangerous," I said. "I think I found our murder weapon. I just need to figure out who used it."

14

Bracken and I continued to follow the path south through the woods.

I was sure I'd guessed right. Violet Layne had told me the crystal ball had a weird effect on magic. Maybe that included latent magical talents for water manipulation. But in order for it to affect him, someone must have pushed him into the water to begin with.

Laurie's death, on the other hand, was likely an accident, but the presence of the crystal ball in the water stirred my suspicions. Now I knew for sure it wasn't Bracken who was responsible, I needed to catch the other elves before they slipped away and took their leader with them. I didn't *think* the elf king would be so easily fooled, but elves were difficult to predict at the best of times.

Maybe one of *them* had thrown the crystal ball into the water. If they had, then well… I hadn't got to that part yet. I was alone in the woods with a drunken elf while my monstrous cat had run away in pursuit of my boyfriend's fairy-hating father who'd just told me my birth mother was dead. To say the situation wasn't entirely within my control was an understatement.

There they are. I stopped at the sight of a pair of short figures standing on the path, not far from where I'd left them before.

"Running away?" I asked the elves.

"Looking for you," Bramble growled. "I heard voices in the woods."

"The werewolf chief's wandering around. You might've forgotten, but this isn't elf territory. Anyway, here's your friend."

Bracken staggered a little behind me, falling against a tree. The effects of the potion must be wearing off. Lucky we'd made it back in time, because carrying him on a broomstick would have been beyond my newly acquired skills.

"How did he get here in this state?" asked Twig.

"Got lucky," I said. "You can have your talk in a minute, but I need to know something first. There's a crystal ball in the water. Did you know about it?"

A moment's pause. "You already questioned us about the crystal ball," said Twig.

"Yes," I said, "but that was before I knew about this." I pulled the shard from my pocket. "Recognise this? It's not just glass. It cancels other magic. Like the ability to breathe underwater or fly on a bewitched broomstick, for instance."

The elves didn't answer.

"Come on," I said. "Did you put this in the water?"

"No," he said.

Lie.

"You know I can sense the truth," I told him. "Tell me. Did you throw this into the water? Or did she?"

"It was not broken before," he growled. "She threw it out of her house, and we saw fit to dispose of it for her. We did her a favour."

I could hardly believe what I was hearing. "It's still cursed with a mixture of enchantments and elf magic, and you went and threw it in a magical lake. What were you thinking?"

"Nobody should have flown that far away from the shore." He fidgeted in an agitated manner. "It was not our intention."

"But two people are still dead," I told him. "Just because you didn't mean for them to die doesn't erase your responsibility."

Bracken got to his feet, looking blearily at the others. "You… you sent Annabel away?"

"They did," I told him. "But I need to ask. Did you intentionally put that crystal ball in the water to cause harm to anyone?"

"No," said Bramble. "Neither of us did, and the first death happened miles from where it was buried."

He was right. Unless both victims had flown directly above the crystal shards, then there was no way to prove the pieces of glass had been responsible. It wasn't an elf who'd committed the murder—but time was still running out.

"Tell him the truth," I told the two elves. "I should add that he's under a spell for clarity and memory, but it's on a time limit. So you might have to tell him twice."

I turned my back on the elves and moved further down the path, now on familiar territory. In no time at all, I reached Annabel's small cottage. Crossing my fingers that she'd be receptive to hearing me out, I knocked on her door.

"Hey," I said, when she answered. "I have good news."

"What?" She scowled, her eyes red-rimmed. "He's leaving town. That's not good news."

"He's not," I said. "I caught him up and explained the situation. Bramble admitted that he and another elf faked the vision you saw in the crystal ball so you'd break up with

Bracken. They broke into your house and used an illusion spell on the enchanted glass."

Her face flushed. "You're lying. That's not just nosy, that's cruel."

"They're telling Bracken the truth now, and they'll be here soon," I said. "He admitted it, Annabel. He said he knew you two planned to get married."

Her eyes closed. "Please, stop."

"Just imagine I'm right. Is it true? He loves you, Annabel."

She swallowed hard. "Elves don't have the same customs as we do, so I asked him how much he knew about their marriage traditions. I wanted to make sure we were on the same page before I asked him for real. That was… that was a week before we ended things."

Long enough for the elves to break into her house and cast their spell on the crystal. It was an inventive plan, I'd give them that. I doubted they'd expected someone to drown in the lake right after they threw away the evidence.

"Annabel, why did you immediately assume you'd developed the gift? When you saw the vision?" I asked. "It's okay, you don't have to tell me, but I wondered."

"Because I already had it," she said quietly. "I lied to my grandmother. When I was younger, I was excited to learn magic. I was impatient, so I borrowed her crystal ball behind her back, and saw—"

"Saw what?"

Annabel sniffed. "I saw… I saw my parents die. They were killed in an accident when I was a kid. That's why my grandmother raised me, but I didn't tell her. I couldn't. Because I saw it and I didn't stop it."

"So you *did* have the gift?" No wonder she'd been so quick to believe the elves' trick. They couldn't possibly have known that, though.

"I don't *want* the gift. I never did." Her voice broke. "When I saw us breaking up, I was scared he'd die, too."

"He's fine," I said. "Well, he's going to have an awful hangover for about a week, but he'll live, and he wants to stay with you. Just keep the faith."

One of us had to.

"Yeah." She sniffed again. "I believe you. Why do I believe you? You're the one who can sense lies, not me."

I pulled the shard of glass from my pocket. "Did you throw this in the lake? I found it in pieces."

"I threw the crystal ball," she said. "It wasn't broken."

"The elves threw it in the lake," I said. "Burying the evidence." In more than one way. I was tempted to report them to the elf king at the very least, but first I had to find a murderer. "And Bracken is on his way here right now."

Her face lit up with hope. Seeing her happiness only drove the shard deeper into my own heart. I gave her a watery smile and turned away. It was time to find out what had really happened that day at the lake.

15

I left Annabel's cottage behind. With any luck, the elves would be on their way with Bracken at their side. Under normal circumstances, I'd stick around to make sure the other two kept their word, but I had a murderer to find. When you took the elves out of the equation, that left the academy students and the sirens. Maybe the High Flier had died by accident or had witnessed the first death, I didn't know, but Terrence's death had started this. Once I found out who killed him, the rest of the details would fall into place.

On my way back to the lake, I gave Helen a call.

"Hey," I said, when she picked up. "I need to talk to the pupils again, is that okay? All the other suspects have been eliminated."

Her breath caught. "All of them? Even the sirens?"

"Well, no, but… they don't have a motive." Though they *did* know the lake, and surely at least one of them would have seen the shattered crystal ball. "But it's not the elves. And I think—"

Helen's voice buzzed to static as a feeling of foreboding

swamped me. I twisted around, gripping my phone with my hand. "Who's there?"

Silence answered. The trees remained quiet and still. Nervous prickles ran up my spine.

"Sky?" I called. I'd sent him to follow Nathan's father. If *he* planned anything, my cat would stop him. But I didn't think it was Mr Harker who was lurking close by. I'd only felt such a weird smothering sensation once before… when I'd looked into the depths of the crystal ball.

I lowered my phone and went for my wand, but sparks flashed behind my head, and the world turned to blackness.

———

I came to when a surge of water crashed over my head. Gasping and spluttering, I fought for breath, as the world reoriented itself. A grassy ledge lay above my head. Someone had magicked me unconscious and pushed me into the water.

"That's *not* cool," I said.

A pair of wet hands grabbed me from behind, yanking me into the depths of the lake.

I kicked out, fighting against the strong grip, but water closed over me, filling my mouth. Gasping, my head broke the surface once again, and I twisted around to look at my attacker.

"You?" I said to the siren. "It was you all along?"

"Sorry," she said. "It's nothing personal, Blair."

Her hands gripped my arms and pulled me under once again. Her grip was like iron, and the air squeezed from my lungs as I fought for breath. She didn't even need to be able to sing to drown me. I kicked out, fighting to keep my head above the surface of the water. She held my arms too tightly for me to grab my wand, but I flailed, my right hand breaking the surface.

I snapped my fingers, turning into fairy mode. My wings beat, breaking her grip, but I couldn't fly underneath the water. I kicked out again—and my wings vanished.

"What the…?"

A glint caught my eye. A piece of crystal, floating in the water. It must have fallen from my pocket. Was it messing with my glamour?

I swam forward, trying to get away from the crystal, but the siren's hands grabbed my ankles, dragging me backwards. I snapped my fingers, and nothing happened. Was the crystal stopping me from changing forms altogether? I flailed and kicked, my arms knocking into a floating stick. No, a broomstick. *My* broomstick. The person who'd tossed me into the lake must have thrown the broom in, too.

I leaned across the water in an attempt to grab it, but the siren's grip was too strong. She let out a guttural snarl, and I cringed, but the crystal must block her siren's song from working.

I gave another kick, wincing as her nails dug into the skin of my ankle. "Why block your *own* powers?"

"I didn't do it on purpose," she snarled. "This was supposed to be easy. You *promised.*"

I frowned at her whining tone and looked up at the bank to see who she spoke to. Casey, Terrence's fellow student. He still wore his academy uniform. He must have sneaked out of school to come here. But *why* was he here?

"*You're* the killer, then?" I gave another kick, and the siren's grip broke long enough for me to lunge for the broomstick.

As my hands closed over its end, the broom's magic kicked in. I hung on as it shot up out of the water, and the siren dove under with a screech when my flailing feet almost hit her in the face.

Casey took a step back. "Don't come near me. I still have this." He held up the shard of glass, and the broom faltered beneath me. As it dropped, I leapt for the bank and landed on the edge.

Casey waved the shard of glass at me. "Don't come near me, Blair, or I'll have to kill you, too."

"You killed Terrence… over the siren, right?" I debated grabbing my wand, but as long as he held the crystal, none of my spells would work. I was trapped between a siren and an unpredictable teenage wizard.

"Not just her." His face was pale, his hands trembling. "He asked Sherry out, too. He always took what was mine."

Careful, Blair. He was unpredictable, but that meant it might be possible to talk sense into him. "Tell me what happened between you."

"I met the siren a few weeks ago," he said. "Terrence tried to talk me out of meeting with her, but he was jealous. And then a couple of weeks ago, she gave me the crystal piece as a present."

"She gave you a piece of broken crystal as a present?" I frowned.

He shrugged. "Well, yeah. I'd been complaining about how Terrence always beat me in class. You know I was meant to be in his place as a Vulture on the Sky Hopper team? But he took that from me, too. I thought about springing the crystal on him during the game. Let him see what it feels like to be humiliated."

Vulture… right, they were the most important team members. I should have remembered the rivalry Helen had mentioned, but it hadn't crossed my mind that a fellow Sky Hopper player might have killed Terrence. "But you used it on him by the lake, right?"

"As a test." His mouth pinched. "I didn't expect it to shut down his magical power."

"So you didn't mean him to drown," I surmised. "But you still meant him harm. And the High Flier, the one who died —the same happened to her, too."

He paled. "Yeah. I didn't know the crystal would still keep working when it was in the water. But we had to cover our tracks. That woman on the broomstick, she spotted one of the pieces of crystal and flew to pick it up…"

"And it cancelled out the spell on her broomstick. But the High Fliers fall into the water all the time and are usually fine." I turned to the siren, who'd emerged from the lake.

"I didn't do it!" she yelped. "The girl drowned because of those ridiculous robes she was wearing. They got caught in the weeds and stopped her from swimming to the surface."

True. Her death had been a genuine accident. Not that the siren wasn't at least partly guilty, considering she'd just tried to drown me.

"We had to cover our tracks," Casey said. "Which means disposing of you, too, Blair."

He held up the crystal shard. It'd stop his own magic from working, but I couldn't use my wand or even my glamour. My wings were locked away. Of all the times not to have my levitating boots… but even *they* might not work.

On the other hand, I did have the element of surprise. And I knew the forest better than he did.

I moved to the left. So did he. His movements were unsure, nervous. He was aware that as long as he held the crystal, he couldn't hex me any more than I could use my own magic against him.

"Get her!" he yelled at the siren. "Drag her back in the lake. Drown her."

The siren shook her head, her glossy hair billowing in the water. "I don't want to hurt anyone else!"

He advanced towards the ledge, not taking his eyes off me. The crystal shard glinted in his hand. If I tackled him, I might be able to take it, but odds were, both of us would fall in.

"I told you to kill her," Casey half yelled at the siren. "It's not that hard."

"You don't have to listen to him," I said to her.

"Yes, she does, because I can block your powers." He waved the crystal shard. "Have you any idea what it's like to always be bottom of the heap?"

"You know, I do," I said. "I've spent most of my life at rock bottom. Also, you know, I might take you more seriously if I hadn't just found out my mother died. Nothing you say or do could ever be worse than that, Casey. Sorry."

His eyes went wide. "Your mother died?"

"Yes." Without warning, I lunged at his free hand, and the crystal shard went flying. I *felt* when its power passed out of range, the rush of freeing power. I snapped my fingers and my wings came out.

The next second, his wand was in his hand. He must have had it up his sleeve all along.

His face contorted, and he took aim at me, but at the same moment, the broomstick took flight, soaring out of the water to the bank. He watched open-mouthed as I grabbed it by the end, swinging wildly and knocking his wand flying out of his hand.

He swore and backed away, but the crystal shard had landed in the water.

"Hand me that crystal back," he commanded.

"I won't!" the siren shouted back. "I won't let you bully me anymore."

"I'm not a bully," he yelled.

"No, you're a murderer." I grabbed my own wand with my free hand. "You and I are going for a little walk to the police station. The *new* one, with its fancy high-security jail. You've seen rock bottom: next you'll get to see a state-of-the-art police facility."

He roared in anger and lunged at me, but before he could make contact, Sky appeared behind him. At the sight of the giant shaggy beast, Casey yelped in alarm, tripping over the ledge into the lake.

I threw the broom in after him as he yelled and thrashed around in the water.

"I'd suggest you hang onto that while I call the…" I trailed off. My phone had been in my pocket when I'd fallen into the water, so calling the police would have to wait. But I'd bet the siren wouldn't help him out this time around.

"Miaow," said Sky, who'd turned back into his cat form.

"Thanks, Sky." I waved my wand and levitated Casey out of the water, then cast a binding spell to tie his hands together. "Can you watch him while I fetch the police?"

"Miaow." Sky padded up to Casey, who paled.

"Don't hurt me, monster cat," he said.

"He eats humans," I told him, giving Sky a grin. he must have known I was in trouble and rushed to help me. Familiar or not, he was loyal to a fault, and he'd probably given Nathan's dad a day to remember.

The quickest way to get someone was through the forest, so I moved in that direction. As I did so, a group of elves emerged from the bushes.

"Blair Wilkes," said the king's guard. "The king requests your presence."

"Not the best timing," I said. "Maybe come back later? I kind of have a murderer tied up here. Unless you're willing to fetch the gargoyles yourself—"

"Miaow," Sky interjected.

"You can do it?" I looked at the elves, then at Casey. After today, I'd be locking myself in my room where nobody could disturb me for a week. "All right. Let's get this cleared up, then."

With the killer in custody, the police wouldn't have reason to throw the blame at the elves. I hoped everyone would stay out of Annabel's and Bracken's way this time. They both deserved that much.

16

I'd much rather take a nap than deal with the elves, but I forced myself to keep moving. After what Nathan's dad had told me, I wasn't sure there was room in my head to accept any more surprises about my family.

We passed between the rows of spear-wielding elves on the way into the elf king's lair. I didn't stop to talk to anyone. I'd also forgotten to cast a drying spell after I got out of the lake, so I left a trail of damp glitter all over the tunnel floor, but nobody commented on it.

The elven king looked down at me as I knelt before him. "I heard you handled the murder investigation without any of my people being locked up, Blair."

"I did. I was waiting for the police to show up when your people brought me here," I said pointedly. "Anyway, you had something to tell me about my family, right?"

"Yes," he said. "We have been communicating with that pixie of yours."

"Wait, you understand him?" If they could, then they knew exactly what my father had said to him. I had only the letters, not the words.

"He's a simple creature, but can be understood," he said. "It seems your father wanted to give you a warning."

"Oh." My brief flash of hope died. "I know. He already sent me a letter. Which I ignored. I'm not leaving the town." Where else was there to go? Besides, I still wanted to learn who my mother had been, even if I had to accept that I'd never get to meet her now. Fairy Falls was my home.

"Not that warning," he said. "He wanted to warn you that if you see or encounter any other fairies, you're not to speak to them."

"Other fairies?" I blinked, confused. "If you mean the sirens, or the nereids…"

"I do not," he said. "He specifically meant other fairies. People like you."

"There aren't any. Not here." Which made his order to leave the town make zero sense. Unless… "Are there other fairies? Coming to town?"

"He didn't tell us," said the elf. "But he asked us to warn you not to speak to them."

"Sure he did." Anger spiked. "I suppose he told you my mother was dead while he was at it."

A moment passed. "Your mother… no. He never mentioned her."

I checked to see if I felt any better. Nope, I didn't. "Well, she's dead. I don't have any other family, do I? That's also what I—I wanted to ask him."

"He didn't mention any, Blair." If my ears weren't deceiving me, there was sympathy in his tone. He also hadn't yelled at me for interrupting. Maybe I was growing on the ill-tempered elf king. "The fairies left this town a long time ago. In other places, too, they went into hiding. But he seemed to believe they're coming back."

The fairies… are coming back?

I didn't know how to feel. The news of my mother's death

had carried my emotions away on its wings, and it'd be a while before I could really process what he was telling me.

"So he told me to leave. Go back to the normals." I shook my head. "And the pixie—*why* tell you and not me? No offence. It's just that I could really have used his help this week."

Then again, the pixie was a magical creature himself. For all I knew, the enchanted glass would have stopped him from flying or worse.

"Pixies are inexplicable creatures," said the elf. "Almost as much as humans are."

Speak for yourself. "So that's it?" I said. "Have you spoken to Bramble and Twig yet?" The two were noticeably absent from the tree-cave—not to mention Bracken, but I'd expected him to still be with Annabel.

"Yes," he answered, his expression shadowing. "They will both face punishment at the court's hands for misuse of magic and endangering human lives. As will Bracken."

"Good," I said. "Wait—Bracken as well?"

"It sounds as though he behaved recklessly."

"I guess," I said, recalling the magical lightning. "But it was mostly those two. They're the ones who dropped the crystal ball in the lake, and it's dangerous to anyone living in there."

The elf king lifted his head. "Yes, it is. I've decided their punishment shall be to swim into the lake and extract all the broken pieces of crystal in person."

"Sounds fitting to me," I said. "Uh—and did you hear the two of them talking about leaving town?"

"They did tell me, after some persuasion," confirmed the elf king. "Absurd, of course. The forest might not be the safest place in existence, but it's our home."

Mutters broke out among the other elves in the cave. One of them spoke up. "Are you sure, your majesty? There have been incidents on our territory lately… just today, two of our people spotted a cat chasing a human out of the woods with a broomstick."

"They spotted a what?" said the elf king, while I tried not to laugh. Oh, Sky. Nathan's family might think twice about paying another visit anytime soon.

Of course, I still had to speak to the man himself… which was another matter entirely.

I cleared my throat. "If you don't need me, I left a murderer tied up by the lake. Can I make sure the police managed to find him?"

———

By the time I reached the lake again, it was to find several gargoyles surrounding Casey. The siren wore handcuffs too, suggesting she'd handed herself in out of guilt. Or Sky had encouraged her to. While he sat in his innocuous cat form on the bank, the way the others avoided him suggested he'd pulled out the monstrous glamour at one point or other. And the broom was still there. Good, because I needed to hand it back over to the witches.

I crouched to pet Sky. "You chased Nathan's dad off?" I murmured. "He's not going to be happy."

"Miaow," said Sky, probably meaning, *I don't care.*

"The elf king said my dad seems to think the fairies are coming here," I whispered to him. "Is he right?"

Sky shook himself, dislodging my hand. He'd been acting weirdly, too, like the pixie. Maybe it was to do with the presence of Nathan's family, but I had a feeling there was more to it than that.

"Blair?" Nathan's deep voice came from behind me.

I swallowed hard. I wasn't ready for this conversation. Especially not here. "Nathan."

"I'm glad you're okay," he said. Sky hissed at him as he tried to take a step closer. "What's your cat doing here?"

"He helped me catch this guy." I waved a hand at Casey, who was sobbing at the gargoyles, his pleas lost under the rustle of wings. "And the siren, too."

"Why didn't you call me?" he asked. "I was worried about you. The police said you went into the forest…"

"To clear things up with the elf king." My throat tightened. He hadn't broached the subject, but maybe he didn't want to discuss his family in front of the crowd. "Er—do you want to talk alone?"

He frowned at Steve, then nodded. "Yes, I think it's best to let the police take over."

I drew in a deep breath and walked with him into the forest, the thick branches closing over our heads. He didn't speak and didn't move to take my hand either. Sky padded at my side, still looking distrustful.

"Sky, don't be absurd," I muttered to him. "This is Nathan, remember? He's safe."

Nathan glanced down at the cat. "He doesn't trust me?"

"He's being a little overprotective," I answered. "Sorry I didn't call. My phone took a swim in the lake."

"How'd that happen?"

I told him. The brief version, anyway. I didn't mention his father, waiting for him to do so, but he listened in silence to my account of how I'd helped Bracken and Annabel and had caught the criminal.

"Really, Blair," he said. "It's a good job your cat was here."

"Yes… when he'd finished chasing your dad away from the woods."

A heartbeat passed. "My father?"

"Yeah, I ran into him on the north side of the lake."

Nathan stopped walking. "You did? What was he doing there?"

"I hoped you could tell me that," I said quietly.

Sky meowed in agreement.

He shook his head. "No. I thought he left town on Sunday night. He made it clear he needed to get back to the office."

Truth. A little of the tension eased out of me, but not all.

"I thought he'd retired," I said.

His brow furrowed. "So did I. But it's not unusual for him to check up on my brother. He doesn't have as much experience as my dad does, and often needs guidance."

I thought of Sky's reaction. "Did either of them mention the fairies coming back to town?"

His gaze slid to me. "No… why? Did someone tell you they were coming back?"

"My dad told the elf king by way of the pixie," I said. "Yeah. They're up to something, and so's your father. He was hanging around by the lake. I don't know what he was doing. But he told me—"

"Don't listen to a word," he said. "I suspected he'd try to get you alone to convince you to break up with me at the first opportunity. He already tried it on me almost every day last week and it didn't work."

But did you know what he told me?

"He told you I was a criminal? That my family was?" I asked.

"Yes, he did. I told you, Blair, I don't see you like that. And you're not a criminal."

"I know I'm not." My voice shook. "My family, though—"

"I can't pretend I know why your father was arrested, but it has nothing to do with you."

"Not him." My voice trembled again, and my eyes burned.

"Blair? What is it?"

He didn't know. *He didn't know.*

I sank down on the forest path, whispering the horrible truth, and Nathan let me cry on him until I was out of tears.

———

Broomsticks wheeled in the air. I tilted my head to watch, gladder than ever that my feet were back on the ground where they belonged.

Helen had picked an empty field at a safe distance from the lake for the academy students to host their Sky Hopper game. While the elves had retrieved all the pieces of broken crystal ball from the lake—aided by the merpeople, who'd grown tired of fishing them out of the depths of the water— the High Fliers and academy students alike mutually agreed that hosting any contest near the lake felt like bad luck.

No more flying for me. I'd passed my test yesterday, and I'd be sticking to wings, wands, and Seven Millimetre Boots from now on. It'd taken some serious pleading with Madame Grey to allow Sky to fly with me, but the witch council had agreed that my wings gave me a disadvantage most other fliers didn't have. They'd unanimously voted to let me bring my cat into my exam. I was lucky to have passed, considering Sky had decided he didn't like flying when we were descending in the final part of the exam and jumped off the broom, landing on one of the examiners' heads in the process.

Helen had bounded up to me the instant I'd received my test scores and pleaded with me to help out at the game, and in a moment of madness, I'd said yes. All I had to do was point my wand into the air and shoot sparks up at the sky to announce each stage of the game. Occasional floods of glitter rained on everyone's heads, but Helen had cheerfully said it created ambience.

Besides, any activity that made me feel normal was more than welcome.

I'd heard nothing more from the pixie, or my dad. While Nathan's family hadn't made a reappearance and Sky was back to his usual enigmatic self, the questions lingered in the back of my mind. The hunters would always be looking for an angle, and I'd bet Nathan's family would be reporting everything they'd seen in Fairy Falls directly to Inquisitor Hare.

As for Nathan… we'd only had the chance to talk a couple of times since my breakdown in the woods. It was clear that me and his family were never going to be on the same page, though he said Erin was already planning to pay me a visit again once she'd secured a new job. She'd left the hunters behind, same as he did. I expected her to show up on Dritch & Co's doorstep any day now.

My co-workers had come out to enjoy the show and clapped along with everyone else when the game finished with Terrence's former team the victors. I raised my wand, fired a streamer of glitter into the air, and applause rang out. Then everyone ducked for cover as the wind caught the glitter, blowing it into their faces.

"Oops," I said.

"You do have a knack for that spell," Bethan commented from behind me, picking glitter out of her hair. On my other side stood Alissa, who grinned.

"I have to be good at something," I said, waving my wand again to make the glitter disappear from our clothes. "Don't think I'll be up in the air like them anytime soon."

"Helen seems to think you will," Alissa whispered.

"Don't even." I looked at the cheering students, and my gaze settled on the group of elves on the other side of the field. Even Bracken and Annabel had come out to watch.

Alissa spotted where I was looking. "Cute," she said in a low voice. "They say they're marrying in winter. It'll be the town's first elf-human wedding."

"And the first fairy-human one will be soon," Bethan added, and I gave her a warning look, glad for once that

Nathan had been too busy to come. He'd taken to walking along the town's northern border himself where possible, but his father hadn't come back.

Alissa nudged me in the ribs. I cringed, expecting to find Nathan behind me listening to every word my gossipy co-workers and best friend said, but it was Madame Grey.

"Blair," she said. "You did a great job. I'm glad to see you getting more involved with our community."

Madame Grey handed out praise even less frequently than Rita did. Naturally, that made me suspicious, and so did the sympathetic expression on her face.

The others moved back to give me space to talk to her. "I owed Helen a favour after helping me learn to ride a broomstick," I explained. "And I wanted to help out the academy, too, since it took me so long to catch the killer. It doesn't hurt to give something back to the town, considering everything you've done for me."

Casey and the siren had both been jailed—the latter with a lighter sentence—and the lake was safe once again. The elves, meanwhile, were under the king's close watch for the foreseeable future.

"You don't owe us anything," she said. "You're always welcome here, Blair. Always. Don't doubt that."

Tears of gratitude stung my eyes. "Thank you. What… what brought this on?"

"Your mother."

My heart did a painful flip. I thought I'd grown used to the notion that she was gone, but every time I remembered, it caught me off guard.

"What about her?" I said quietly.

"We've been digging into the town's history," she said. "My fellow coven leaders and I, that is. When she left, we all assumed she'd gone to a different paranormal community away from here. But what you told us… it paints the situation in a new light."

You're telling me. I'd told Rita what I'd learned, and she'd passed it onto Madame Grey. I didn't know how I'd managed to pass my exam considering how distracted I'd been, but my wand practical had been put on hold until my emotions were back under some semblance of control.

"Your mother was by all accounts a remarkable witch," Madame Grey said. "But a criminal… no. Certainly not while she lived here."

"Nathan's dad worked for the hunters," I whispered to her. "If anyone knew, he did. And—and you heard Blythe's mother. She said the same. And she didn't lie."

Her mouth tightened. "Perhaps. We'll continue to look into it."

It did make me feel much better to know Madame Grey didn't believe my mother was a criminal. Sure, Blythe's mother believed so, but my lie-sensing power wasn't faultless. Recent events proved that, at least.

"Has anyone mentioned fairies coming back to the falls?" I asked her.

"No. Why?"

"Just something I heard. From the elves." She didn't know about the pixie, or my dad, and now wasn't the time to bring up the subject. Dad hadn't wanted me to tell her, but considering recent events, maybe he'd have a change of heart if I explained she was on my mother's side.

"If we had, I would know," she said. "The elves do talk to us, you know. They're not as insular as they appear."

"I thought they didn't deal with the witches at all." I was starting to think Bramble had wanted me to believe that on purpose. But while he and Twig had tried their best to prevent Annabel and Bracken from finding happiness together, they'd failed.

"I think we know that's about to change, Blair." Her gaze went to the happy couple. I caught Annabel's eye and she smiled at me across the field. "But don't let a few rumours ruin your memory of your mother. I have no doubt she loved you."

My eyes stung again. Maybe she had, but it didn't change the fact that I'd never see her again.

"I think she did," I murmured. "I also think she didn't mean for me to find this world at all."

"And do you regret it?" Her eyes were kind, and I became conscious of the clamour surrounding me. The broomsticks landing as the triumphant students talked excitedly. My friends and co-workers gathered close by, ready to support me no matter what happened.

"No," I said. "No regrets here."

From the instant I'd arrived in Fairy Falls, I'd known I was in for a bumpy ride. My relationship with Nathan was no exception to that rule. But there was proof right in front of me that I didn't have to let others' opinions rule the choices I made.

Even a seer couldn't know everything that was to come. The future wasn't set in stone, not for any of us. But that was part of the fun.

ABOUT THE AUTHOR

Elle Adams lives in the middle of England, where she spends most of her time reading an ever-growing mountain of books, planning her next adventure, or writing. Elle's books are humorous mysteries with a paranormal twist, packed with magical mayhem.

She also writes urban and contemporary fantasy novels as Emma L. Adams.

Find Elle on Facebook at https://www.facebook.com/pg/ElleAdamsAuthor/